Chapter One

SAMANTHA WINTERS KNEW SHE was a bad person. Her sister spit out a mouthful of sand, and Sam couldn't stop laughing. Maddie glared at her, but Sam just rolled back on her elbows and raised her face skyward. The sun was warm on her skin, a soft breeze ruffled her hair, and she had an ice cold diet Dr. Pepper by her side. Life was good. After the shit couple of months she'd had, she needed this.

Maddie picked up her frisbee and jumped to her feet. At fifteen, she was just coming into her long legs and had all the grace of a baby giraffe. She brushed sand off her bathing suit with a sheepish grin before tossing the frisbee to one of her friends.

Sam raked her fingers through the end of her chestnut ponytail. It had been only a month since Maddie had left the hospital, and it was nice seeing her so happy again. Her sister's smiles had become more and more infrequent the past year, but this day at the beach seemed to be just what she needed.

"Hey, sorry we're late."

Sam shaded her eyes Her best friend, Caroline, tromped through the sand toward her, a beach chair wedged under one arm. Her boyfriend, Jake, took it from her hands, snapped it open, and plopped it in the sand next to Sam's.

"Hi, Caroline. Hey, Jake. I'm glad you guys could make it." Sam pulled her tank top strap back onto her shoulder.

"Some fun in the sun, followed by s'mores around a fire pit?" Jake stabbed the end of a beach umbrella into the sand before cranking it open. "Wouldn't miss it."

Sam carefully directed her gaze away from the flexing muscles in Jake's arms. While he was a tasty treat, he was Caroline's eye candy now. Her friend had hit the jackpot when it came to her love life. Jake was a Marine Raider, a special forces operative for the military, and he had the elite body to match his elite job. But beyond being nice to look at, he was also a stand-up guy who adored her friend.

Sam smiled. *Lucky bitch.* She really was happy for her friend.

"Heads up," a man shouted.

Jake turned, but not fast enough to stop a tote bag from smacking into his chest. Towels spilled from the bag when it hit the sand.

"Asshole," Jake muttered, bending for the towels.

Chris Gunn, the one coworker of Jake's Samantha prayed she wouldn't see, strolled up next to them and stretched. His black hair glinted in the sunlight. "What a great day."

Sam looked behind him, but no other big, brawny man appeared. Only Jake and Chris. Jake, at least, was a welcome addition. But if Chris was going to be here, Sam needed more people as a buffer. She caught Caroline's eye and tipped her head to the unwanted guest.

Sorry, Caroline mouthed. She shrugged, her pale hair sliding over her shoulder. "We invited the rest of the guys, but they had other plans."

"Ryan might show." Jake settled a large cooler on a towel under the umbrella. He adjusted the umbrella, making sure shade covered the cooler.

"Ryan has shown." A blond-haired Adonis joined them. He made a sweeping bow. "At your service."

"Oh, thank God." Sam grinned up at the other member of Jake's squad. "I thought I was going to be stuck"—*with Chris*—"as the third-wheel with Jake and Caroline."

Chris scowled. "What the hell am I?"

"An annoyance." Ryan pulled a football from his duffel bag and pointed it at Sam. "How about some catch? You've got the legs of a wide-receiver."

"Thanks?" She didn't know if that was an insult or compliment. Either way, getting physical with the tech guru of the squad was an appealing option. With his ripped muscles, blue eyes, and square jaw, Ryan was the epitome of all-American good looks. She wished that she felt something other than a friendly interest in the man, but so far, they were spark-less.

Chris snorted. "She can't throw a spiral to save her life. It's best if she stays on the cheerleader squad."

Sam's shoulders inched toward her ears. God, how she wished the Raiders were four-man teams. What did Chris bring to the special forces unit anyway? An over-sized ego and copious amounts of sarcasm?

Sam pasted an encouraging smile on her face. "I know you derive your self-worth from your ability to throw a ball, but I'm sure there's something else you're good at." She cocked her head and looked up and down his body. She kept a disinterested look on her face, but her skin heated. He was over six feet of chiseled muscle, with jet black hair, deep blue eyes, and a sexy cleft in his chin.

The bastard *would* have a chin dimple. They were one of her many downfalls.

She tossed her ponytail over her shoulder. "I haven't noticed any other talents yet, but they must be there somewhere."

Jake and Ryan hooted.

Chris pushed his sunglasses to the top of his head, his deep blue eyes glittering. He stomped to the umbrella and tugged on the towel pinned beneath the cooler, yanking it free. Sand flew at Sam.

She tried to shield herself with her arm, but it was too late. She spit out sand and jumped to her feet. "Watch it, moron."

He widened his eyes innocently. "Sorry. I guess that's something else I'm not talented at."

She shook out her shorts and tank, growling. She opened her mouth to lay into him, but saw Caroline chewing on her bottom lip like it was saltwater taffy.

Sam sighed. Caroline hated it when she fought with Chris. She wanted to meld her two worlds together, her boyfriend, and his friends, with her friends.

Sam gritted her teeth. "No problem," she said to Chris. She plopped back in her chair. In a low voice, she said so only Caroline could hear, "I'm only biting my tongue because you were close to death this year." A clammy shiver raced down her spine, remembering just how close she'd come to losing her friend.

"And I appreciate it. For almost being murdered, how long do I get Nice Sam?"

"Another three months. Tops." Her anger cooled as she remembered Caroline's trouble. Her friend had been targeted by the son of the leader of a Columbian cartel. Sam swallowed. She'd almost lost her a couple of times. The only good thing that had come out of that whole experience was that Caroline had met Jake.

Chris peeled off his shirt, leaving him in swim trunks and a smirk. Jake and Ryan followed suit, and Sam and Caroline exchanged a look. They were surrounded by more muscles than Sam typically saw during an entire afternoon at the gym. Chris stretched, his tan skin pulling taut. His trunks sank low on his hips, revealing that Y indentation framing his lower abdomen that only a gazillion sit-ups and the genetics of an angel could produce.

Or a devil.

Drool pooled in Sam's mouth, and she swallowed. It wasn't fair that the most annoying member of Jake's squad had to be the hottest. She wondered what all that muscle and sinew would feel like under her hands. If—

"See something you like?" He bunched his shirt and tossed it toward his bag.

"Yeah." Sam cleared her throat. "A diet soda. You're blocking the cooler." She rose and skirted around him, not wanting to touch him but kind of hoping she'd brush his body, too. Clearly, Chris wasn't the only moron here. What did it make her if she was attracted to one? "You want one, Caroline?"

Maddie jogged up, greeting Caroline and the guys. Her friends from high school, Bailey and Jayden, followed after. "Hey," Maddie said, flicking her ponytail behind her. Her hair was the same chestnut color as Sam's. "We're going in the water to cool off."

"Careful." Sam took the frisbee Jayden handed her and dropped it by her chair. "I overheard some people talking about an aggressive seal in the water today."

Jayden snorted. "Aggressive seals? Not something anyone's going to make a horror movie about."

Sam arched her eyebrows. To be fifteen again and think that nothing could ever hurt you. "Seals are large animals with equally large teeth. Like any wild animal, they can bite." Though now that she thought about it, she didn't think she'd ever heard of a seal attack in North Carolina.

But it *could* happen. And this was her little sister and her friends. It was Sam's job to protect them. Or at least give them a warning.

Maddie looked at her expectantly.

"Go on." Sam waved them away. "But you should reapply your sun..." Her sister and friends were gone before she could finish the word. "...screen."

Chris stepped next to her. "Is Maddie gone already? I wanted to play some volleyball with her and her friends."

Sam blew out a breath. Even though she couldn't stand the man, he did have one redeeming feature. He was good with her sister. In fact, he liked Maddie's company more than hers. Which was fine. And with the trouble her sister had been in lately, the girl could use all the friends she could get.

Sam turned and patted Chris on the arm, trying to ignore the way his muscles flexed under her fingers. "You'll just have to find some boys and girls your own age to play with," she told him.

Chris narrowed his eyes.

Sensing a disturbance in the force, Caroline sidled between them and wove her arm through Sam's. "I saw an ice cream cart up on the boardwalk. Come get some with me." Without waiting for Sam's response, Caroline dragged her away before any fights could start.

"If this is you biting your tongue, I'm scared what's going to come out of your mouth when my three months are up," Caroline said.

"It's not my fault," Sam explained. "He provokes me. You should be impressed that I haven't stabbed him through the eyeball with my car keys."

Caroline gave her the side-eye. "Thought about that a lot, have you?"

Sam sighed. "Every time I see him."

"Then I am impressed with your self-restraint." She smiled at the ice cream man. "Do you want a vanilla or chocolate ice cream sandwich? I'm buying."

"Chocolate." Sam unwrapped the treat and licked around the edges. It was nice being rewarded for good behavior. She should make a point of telling her friend every time she refrained from stabbing someone.

"So how's it going with Maddie living with you?" Caroline bit into her own sandwich. "It seems like Maddie staying with you for a couple of days has now become permanent."

Sam turned back to the beach, heading in the opposite direction of the guys. "It's going good. I think. There are still days of sulkiness and anger, but there are more days now like today. Where she's happy. I think...." She stopped walking. The surf crawled up the shore, brushing her toes before retreating. "I think it's good she's out of my mom's house. How can I tell Maddie how stupid it was to do drugs when she sees Mom drinking every night?"

Maddie's overdose had been a wake-up call for Sam. She'd known her mom had stopped being a good parent a long time ago, but she'd let Maddie stay in the house, thinking it wasn't her right to get between her sister and her mom.

But it hadn't been right to let Maddie live in that environment. Sam had hoped when her mom had remarried three years ago that her new husband, Frank, would have been a good influence. He didn't drink to excess and had a steady job. He wasn't Sam's favorite person, but her mom could have done a lot worse.

After Maddie had left the hospital, Sam had told her mom that she would stay with her for a few days. Sister-time. But that had extended to weeks now, and Sam wasn't in any rush to send Maddie back home.

"You can use your mother as an example of how Maddie shouldn't waste her life." Caroline twisted her lips. "Sorry, she's still your mom, I know."

Sam finished her ice cream bar and folded the wrapper, putting it in her pocket until she came across a garbage can. "It's too nice a day to talk about this crap. I want a new topic." She waggled her eyebrows. "So, when do you think Jake is going to pop the question?" It was only partly a joke. Jake and Caroline had only been seeing each other for a couple of months, but Sam knew how quickly their relationship had gotten serious. It wouldn't surprise her if Jake did intend to lock her friend down.

Caroline shook her head. "I am in no rush. Things are going so great right now, I..." Her forehead wrinkled. "Maddie, what's wrong?"

Sam's sister sprinted up to them, panting. She pressed her hand to her side. "Riptide," she gasped out. She pointed to the water. "Bailey and Jayden couldn't get out."

Sam forced herself to remain calm. Panicking was the worst thing a person could do when in trouble on the water. That was one of the things she'd learned from her lifeguard training when she'd been a teenager.

She gripped her sister's shoulders. "Do you see that lifeguard station back there?" She pointed down the beach where the shack stood about a quarter mile off. "Run there and tell them what happened. I'll go help your friends."

Madison nodded and took off.

"Sam—" Caroline started.

"Go with her." Sam pushed her friend in Maddie's direction. Without waiting for a response, she took off, pounding across the hard-packed sand. The current was pulling Jayden and Bailey north along the coast. About fifty feet of water separated the two friends.

Sam's pulse raced. Rescuing two victims in differing locations wasn't optimal, to say the least. But these were kids Sam knew. She'd met their parents. She had to do whatever she could for them, and hope the lifeguards would be there soon to help.

She dragged her tank top up and over her head as she ran. She should take off her shorts, too, swim in only her bathing suit to reduce drag, but she didn't want to waste the time it took. Her feet splashed in the surf.

Something gripped the top of her shorts and yanked her backwards.

Sam shrieked, stumbling to a stop.

"Stay here," Chris ordered. He ran past her and dove into the break. His arms sliced through the water, his aim taking him towards Bailey.

Sam shielded her eyes. Jayden was further up off the shore. She took off running again, wanting to get as close to his position as possible before she started swimming.

A young boy wearing plastic blue flippers high-stepped it into the ocean, carrying a boogie board.

She splashed over to the kid, grabbed the boogie board, and yanked.

The boy's thin arms were stronger than they looked. He yanked back. "This is mine."

"I need it for a water rescue. Someone's in trouble." She pointed into the sea. Jayden waved frantically. His head dipped under the water before popping back up.

"I don't care. It's mine." The boy dropped his chin and glared.

Oh for.... She didn't have time to argue. She wrestled the foam board from his grip and took off. "Don't be selfish!" she called over her shoulder before launching herself up and over a wave. Her abdomen landed on the board, and she started swimming. It wasn't as aerodynamic as a surfboard and she only seemed to inch closer to Jayden.

She should have stolen the kid's flippers, too.

A wave smacked her in the face. Jayden's panicked shouts reached her ears. She pulled harder through the water, ignoring the ache in her arms.

He was coughing up water when she reached him. She slid off the board and pushed it toward him.

Jayden grabbed it. Instead of laying on top, he tried to climb aboard. His knee pushed it under the water, and he went face-first back into the ocean.

Sam pushed the board to him again. "Stop fighting. Hold onto it and lay still."

She didn't think he heard her. His gaze darted about wildly. He pushed the board beneath the water again.

Damn it. Swimming closer, she reached for the teenager.

His flailing arm caught her on the cheek. He tried to wrap his arms around her, but she kept the board between them, knowing in his panic he could drown the both of them.

"Jayden! You need to calm down. You need—"

A figure cut through the water next to her, circling the board on her right.

Another swimmer came up on her left. "Are you all right?" Jake asked.

"Yes, but Jayden—"

"Ryan's got him." He nodded to his friend who had wrapped up the teenage boy, restraining his arms, as he spoke softly to him.

Jake reached for the boogie board and handed it to her. "Use this to get back."

"But with Jayden, shouldn't Ryan use it?"

Jake prodded her onto the board. "He's a strong swimmer. He'll get the boy back safe."

Indeed, Ryan had already swum past them, heading for the shore, Jayden in one arm.

"Bailey?"

Jake grabbed the board's leash and kicked out, going with the current for a few strokes before angling toward the beach. "Chris has her. Don't worry, my men are good at what we do. Now let's get you in."

Sam nodded. Not wanting it to look like she needed a rescue, she dug in, kicking as hard as she could until the leash went slack and she was abreast of Jake.

"You could just enjoy the ride," Jake said.

Sam huffed in response.

He grinned. "Good. I hate acting like a tug boat." He dropped the leash, but stayed next to her all the way in.

Two lifeguards met them in the shallows, one of them helping her to her feet.

Sam bent over at the waist, trying to catch her breath. She used to swim every day. By the way she was panting now, she was way out of practice.

She scanned the beach. Bailey was sitting cross-legged in the sand further up, drinking from a water bottle.

Jayden was ten feet down from her. He looked calmer, but his iron-clad grip on Ryan's shoulder told of his fright.

But he was breathing. Alive.

Sam's knees went soft. She hoped it looked like the tide made her stumble as she wobbled onto the firm sand.

Everyone was okay. She took a deep breath. Another. This would probably end up making a good story for the kids to tell their friends. She blocked her mind from thinking about how else this day might have ended.

Chris jogged toward them, followed by Caroline and Madison. When Chris reached her, he grabbed her arms and gave her a small shake. His eyes scanned her body. "What the hell were you thinking? I told you to stay put."

Sam's body tensed. "What, in our short history, made you think that I would take orders from you?"

His fingers dug into her arms. "Maybe you could give your ego a rest and follow the advice of someone trained at rescues."

Advice? That was a laugh. Only Chris would think that demanding someone stay like a dog could be considered advice.

She shook off his grip. "I'll have you know I was a lifeguard."

He snorted. "In summer camp? Or did you watch the kiddies in the local pool at the rec?"

Heat swept up Sam's body, scorching her cheeks. "There was a big lake at summer camp. I'll have you know—"

She exhaled noisily. There was no point in arguing with someone like Chris. "I had everything under control with my rescue," she said tightly.

Jake came up, his arm slung around Caroline's shoulders. "She's a strong swimmer. And you were smart to use the board," he said, turning to Sam.

"Thank you." Although she hadn't been able to secure Jayden before Ryan and Jake showed up. But Chris didn't need to know that.

"We're trained in water rescues. There were lifeguards on duty." Chris shook his head. "You were stupid to go out there yourself."

"I'll make a deal with you." Sam stepped forward and poked him in the chest. "If you are ever in need of rescuing, I'll make sure to stay on the beach and leave you to your fate."

Chris narrowed his eyes. A lock of dark hair clung to his forehead, a bead of water rolling from it.

Sam had the strangest urge to brush it back. She stepped away quickly. "Now, if you'll excuse me, I have a boogie board to return." She took the board from the lifeguard holding it and stalked up the beach, hoping to get to the kid before he called the cops on her.

Chapter Two

CHRIS CLICKED THE TOP of his pen on and off, on and off. He and the rest of his MSOT, Marine Special Operations Team, were in a conference room on base. The full 14-man team was here, all four HQ leaders and both five-man tactical squads.

Captain Gifford ran his fingers through his steel-gray hair. His slight paunch strained the buttons of his khaki shirt. The man had been trying his best to lose a few pounds rather than order another uniform a size up. "It hasn't been decided yet whether Alpha"—he nodded at Jake, their squad's element leader—"or Delta"—he looked at the other squad—"will be deployed for this mission. But I want both of you to be ready to go wheels-up by end of week."

Chris's skin hummed the way it always did when they were on the knife's edge of a mission. He'd joined the Raiders knowing this was the best place for him to serve his country, but he couldn't deny the rush he got from his job.

"Even though the host nation is aware we'll be coming, you'll land in Djibouti under the cover of night," the captain continued. "We don't want our presence broadcast."

Chris made a note to himself to start boning up on his French and Arabic. Each Raiders' squad consisted of their Element Leader, Jake for their squad. There was also a Navy Special Reconnaissance Corpsman trained in advanced trauma management. Tony Garcia held that position for Alpha. The rest of the five-man team was filled with three Critical

Skills Operators. The CSOs were intensively trained to become experts in different subject matters, and Chris's specialties were intelligence and foreign languages. Ryan Kelly was their advanced communications CSO, and Travis Kowalski was trained in special weapons. Together, the five of them formed one hell of a kick-ass special forces squad, if Chris did say so himself.

He raised his hand and Captain Gifford nodded at him. "Yes, Corporal Gunn."

"Will we be working alone or jointly with another SOCOM team?"

"Special Operations Command might send SEAL Team Eight to join in the fun but that's not confirmed. Anyone else?" The captain scanned the room then nodded when no one else spoke up. "That's it for now." He closed the binder on the podium in front of him and strode from the room.

The rest of the guys gathered their things. Chris stood and stretched.

"Our monthly assessment is coming up in a couple of days." Jake nodded to Delta squad as they filed past. His jade green eyes glowed under the florescent lights. "I want to do a run through for our PT."

Tony groaned. Each month every Raider was tested for physical fitness and the session was grueling. From suicide shuttle sprints to sled pushes and pull-ups, the assessment monitored each man's power, speed, and agility, ensuring they were optimally prepared for the job.

Chris bumped Tony's shoulder as he walked past. "What's the matter, Frogman? Can't handle a little PT with the big boys?"

"Don't tell me you're excited about this?" Tony asked, blinking.

Chris shrugged. He didn't necessarily enjoy the monthly hell that had been known to make some grown men cry, but it was a challenge he looked forward to. He wanted to get better times, set heavier weight records each assessment. It was a good tool to measure his improvements.

"Chris is just our little eager beaver, when it comes to PT." Travis crumpled up a piece of note paper and tossed it at him. "Maybe that should be his call sign. Beaver." He snorted.

"No." Chris tried to put as much authority into his voice as he could. It wasn't up to him to choose his nickname. Call signs were given to a servicemember with or without their consent. All the other men in Alpha had been given their designations; only Chris remained nickname-less. But there was no way in hell he'd let himself be saddled with *Beaver*.

Tony and the rest of the guys followed him out into the hallway and over to the gym. "Well, I have a date tonight," Tony said. "And I'd like to be able to do more than move my mouth. I know you don't care about pleasuring a woman, but I like to put my best into it."

Travis snorted. "If you don't know how much can be done with just a mouth, then I seriously doubt your ability to please a woman, Viper."

Tony swept Travis's leg, the scuffle drawing a long-suffering sigh from Jake and a chuckle from Ryan.

Chris tuned them out, thinking about his own last date. It...hadn't gone well. How could it when every time he'd moved in to kiss Sandra another woman's face had appeared in his mind? One with a full bottom lip, flushed cheeks, and eyes that spit sparks. But maybe that was just the way Sam looked when he was around. She never seemed to open that pretty mouth except to insult him. He never thought he was the kind of guy who'd look forward to a tongue-lashing, but he got hard every time they argued.

Except for when she argued with him about her safety.

Chris frowned. She'd been an idiot, jumping into the ocean with a known rip current when there were three high-ly-trained men available for the rescue, plus professional life-guards on duty.

The image of her coming out of the ocean, her tiny shorts molded to her ass and thighs, water beading on the tops of her breasts, invaded his mind. He huffed out a breath. And now he was right back to wanting her.

Samantha Winters drove him crazy. She was sexy and annoying in equal measures. His brain was either in fuck or fight mode with her, and since she hadn't shown any inclination to actually have sex with him, that meant they did a whole lot of fighting.

He opened his locker and pulled out gym clothes. But at night, in his dreams, he let himself imagine how it would be between them. He'd explored every inch of her toned body in his mind. Sam was athletic, her curves subtle, understated, yet still all woman.

He changed into the shorts and tee. He'd probably never know if his imaginings matched reality. It was better that way. She was best friends with Jake's girlfriend, and that presented too many complications.

Jake closed his locker, the sound dragging Chris from his thoughts. "Caroline wants to go out tonight so we're heading to *The Limber Ginger* after work. Sounds like Tony's busy, but will you guys be there? We can sit at another table if having Caroline there will cramp your style."

Which meant Jake didn't want the rest of the guys making out with some waitress on their lap while his girl was at the table.

Ryan grabbed towels from the closet and tossed one to each of them. "We'll behave. Tell Caroline to bring her friends." He hung his own towel around his neck. "I know Chris has Sam, but Caroline has to have more hot friends."

Chris's jaw dropped. "Excuse me, what? In what way do I have Sam? She's like the annoying little sister I'm glad I never had." He'd never, not once, admitted his attraction for Sam to the guys, and all they'd ever seen him and Sam do was fight.

Travis snorted. "If you look at annoying little sisters the way you do at Sam, it's a good thing you never had one. That would have been effed up. And illegal."

Tony nodded. "You do spend most of your time eye-fucking her when she's around."

The back of his neck went hot. "That's bullshit. She's irritating, loud, and pig-headed."

"Smoking hot ass, though," Ryan said. "That makes up for a lot."

Chris clenched his hands. "Watch your mouth," he growled.

Ryan shared a look with the other guys, his grin widening. "Protecting her honor now? Yeah, he's not into her at all."

Chris slammed the door to his locker. It banged back open, and he slammed it again. "You all are a bunch of assholes."

"But they're not wrong." Jake grabbed his duffle bag and headed for the door to the gym. "Just be careful with this one. If she goes crying to Caroline, Caroline will come to me. I don't want to be involved in your relationships."

"There *is* no relationship."

Jake glanced over his shoulder. "Probably best to keep it that way. I have a feeling the two of you together would be nothing but trouble."

Chris bit his tongue. He wanted to ask if this was just a normal feeling, or a *feeling*-feeling. Jake's nickname of Psych wasn't a joke. The man had a sixth sense, a strong intuition when things were about to get squirrely. It had saved their asses more than once.

But it didn't matter. Chris had his own reasons for avoiding any entanglements, and Sam was already one thorny-ass knot. She wasn't the type of woman who would enjoy a nice hate-fuck then walk away with a smile on her face. She was a forever type of woman, the kind who would eventually want the white picket fence and a yard full of kids.

He headed for the pull-up bar, looking forward to the burning muscles the next couple hours would bring. Stressing his body helped clear his mind, and on one point he needed absolute focus.

Yes, Sam was a forever kind of woman.

And that was something he could never give.

Chapter Three

SAM TUCKED THE OFFICE phone between her shoulder and ear, her eyes focused on her computer screen.

"The mayor said that the benches in Willingham Park would be replaced," the woman on the other end said. "Well, they've been taken away but nothing's come back to replace them."

Sam's fingers flew over the keyboard as she responded to an email. "Those benches are still being repaired. They'll be back, Helen."

She moved to the next email, only partially paying attention to the call. Helen was one of those citizens who actually gave a damn, and called the mayor's office whenever she saw a problem with the city's management. She'd had nearly the same conversation with her last week, and the week before....

Helen sniffed. "And then there was that nonsense with taping off the other benches for several months. I had nowhere to rest during my walks."

Sam winced. That hadn't been the city's finest moment. "It was for social distancing," she said weakly. She wished the older woman wasn't such a stickler for following the rules. She should have just done what everyone else had. Torn away the painters' tape and taken a seat if she'd needed to.

Leaning back, Sam gazed at the stained tiled ceiling of her office at city hall. She liked her job working as a communications associate for the mayor, but sometimes she felt like she was the black hole where every grievance and complaint in Jacksonville was sent to die. And it wasn't like she actually made any of the decisions the people complained about. She just took all the heat for them.

"I promise," Sam said, "it is still in the budget to have these benches replaced. If something changes, I'll let you know."

"Hmf. That's the same answer I got last week, but I guess it's better than nothing." A timer dinged over the phone line. "I'm baking shortbread cookies," Helen said. "You and Maddie should come up after work and I'll have a baggie for you."

Sam's lips tugged upwards. But there were definitely benefits with this particular complainer. When she'd discovered that the Helen who was the scourge of the mayor's office lived in her building, she'd thought she'd be getting a knock on her door every day about city issues. But Helen had turned out to be a good neighbor, and a very nice lady.

"Maddie and I will see you tonight. Later, Helen." She placed the receiver back in its cradle and stretched.

Her coworker, Casey Greenberg, leaned back in his chair and ran his hand down his lime green tie. "I don't know how you stay so patient with that one. She must drive around the city every day looking for problems."

Sam opened up another email and shrugged. Aside from the mayor's personal office and some conference rooms, the rest of the space was an open floor plan, each employee given a low cubicle that afforded zero privacy. Every conversation was overheard. "She's concerned about her city." On the whole, Sam preferred the people who were more interested in their city than those who didn't seem to give a damn.

She forwarded an email to the mayor, deleted two others, and saved one that she would respond to herself tomorrow. Delete. Forward. Respond.... Her hand paused on the mouse.

Casey strolled over and cocked his hip on her desk. His narrow-legged slacks showcased toned calves and thighs, and a nervously bouncing leg. "I've got tickets to a Turkish Beatles cover band."

"Sounds like an interesting combo." Sam leaned forward, peering at the latest email. This one was a tough call. Definitely angry but didn't contain any overt threats unless she read between the lines. It was probably nothing. People were always angry at the mayor. She blew out a breath. Hell, she'd send it on to the PD just to be safe. Someone else, someone who was paid more, could make the decision about whether the mayor was being threatened here.

"Uh, so do you want to go?" Casey asked. He looked at her hopefully. "It's tomorrow night."

Sam shifted in her chair. She knew Casey was interested in her, and on paper he was a great match. He was cute, with a trim build and the type of face that would look young even when he was 50. They had similar interests and worked well together. But she never felt a spark with him.

Heat flushed through her body at the memory of Chris grabbing her shorts, pulling her back on the beach, then racing into the water. She bit her lower lip. His muscles had bunched and flexed with a calm determination as he'd swam for her sister's friend.

Her lower belly quivered. Damn it, why did there have to be a spark between her and *him*? She could usually channel that heat into a much healthier emotion – like a rage that could fry Corporal Christopher Gunn into ash. He was demanding, after all. Obnoxious. Presumptuous, thinking he could tell her what to do. He was always picking at her, finding flaws with everything she did.

She sighed. But they had a definite spark.

She turned off her computer. Anger at herself made her face go hot. She had a great guy here in front of her, but it was that big lumbering oaf that got her motor running. An absolute asshat who her body wanted to climb like a tree.

Her shoulders slumped. Sometimes life just wasn't fair. "I can't," she told Casey. "Maddie has a game that night, but thanks for thinking of me." She pulled her purse from her bottom drawer. "Oh, look at the time. Gotta go."

She scurried out of there, looking anywhere but at his face. She hated disappointing people, and telling a guy she just didn't see him that way was more emotional effort than she wanted to put in tonight.

She called goodbye to the other city employees she passed on her way out of the building and pushed out the double doors. Her Honda Civic was across the parking lot, and she trotted over to it, wanting to make it inside before Casey left and asked her out for another night.

She dropped her keys in front of her door, because, of course. The scent of cigarettes invaded her nose as she bent to retrieve them. She hurried inside her car and slammed the door, blocking out the odor. Turning the engine, she headed home, happy that this day was finally over.

She merged onto the highway, joining the rush hour crowd. Even in Jacksonville, North Carolina, they had traffic. It seemed inescapable, like taxes, and the fact she was never going to fit back into her high school jeans.

Turning on the radio, she sang along, letting the music relax her muscles.

Until her engine lurched, stuttered, and died. Then her muscles clenched again. "Shit." She checked her mirrors and drifted into the right lane.

A car behind her blared its horn.

Sam stomped on the gas pedal, but her car didn't magically come to life again. There was a shoulder, but it wasn't big. A concrete barrier loomed to her right. She managed to get most of her car off the highway before it stopped rolling.

"Damn it." She slapped her hand on the wheel. She did not need another bill. Things had always been tight, but now with Maddie living with her, it could come down to paying for her car to be fixed or paying for rent.

She pulled the hood release lever. Maybe it would be something obvious that she could fix. A doohicky out of place. A thingamajig that just needed refilling. Anything more complex than that and she was SOL.

She opened her door and put one foot to the ground.

A horn screamed. Headlights blinded her.

With a shriek, she jumped back inside, slamming the door. Her heart hammered as a Jeep bulleted past her, inches from her car.

Blinking furiously, she willed the tears not to fall. She was not a crier. She hadn't even cried when her dad had died, knowing she needed to be the rock for her mom and sister. She swiped her fingers across her damp cheeks. But over the past year, she'd started to feel overwhelmed. First with her sister acting out, then the horrible night Maddie had tried drugs at a party and ended up in the hospital, and now with her living in the same apartment.

Sam loved having her sister with her, but she had the crawling suspicion that she might have taken on more responsibility than she could handle.

She took several deep breaths. Checking her mirrors, she waited until the lane next to her was clear and darted out and around the front of her car. She was on the shoulder, but she still didn't feel safe. Other cars were going much too close and much too fast. There was no way she was opening the hood and standing out here like a target, pretending she could fix her car.

She hurried down the shoulder until it widened. The concrete barrier dropped away. She scurried into the grasses next to the road until she felt far enough away a car wouldn't hit her.

She snorted. Now all she had to worry about was a wild animal coming up from behind and making her its dinner.

She forced her brain to stop its twisted imaginings. She was a capable adult. She'd be fine.

But her hand still trembled as she pulled out her phone to call for help.

Chapter Four

"WRENCH." JAKE'S VOICE WAS muffled, bent as he was under the bathroom vanity.

Tony reached into the dented toolbox on the toilet and handed him one.

Chris and Tony were at Jake's and Caroline's house helping with a bathroom remodel. Chris had somehow been roped into it when they'd been at the bar the night before. He didn't know when Jake had suckered Tony into it. But free food had been promised for after they were done.

"Screwdriver. Flathead." Jake held out his hand, his head still buried under the sink.

"Scalpel, please." Chris leaned against the door jamb. "You make a very good nurse, Viper."

Tony scowled. "You could get your ass in here and help, too. Don't want to break a nail, princess?"

"I'm supervising." Chris narrowed his eyes. Tony had better not become too comfortable calling him princess. That *was not* going to be his call sign. Besides, he'd helped plenty and now was just waiting to get in there and paint. "And it's too damn small for three people in there."

Jake pulled his head out of the vanity and sat back on his haunches. "Hence the remodel job." He lifted his T-shirt to wipe his forehead. "I'm hoping to give Caroline a little more space in here."

"This new sink has a lot more storage than her old one." Tony tapped the new shelves built between the studs in the wall. "And this recessed shelving I put in should help with your space issue."

Jake arched an eyebrow. "That you put in?"

"I definitely did at least sixty percent of the work," Tony argued.

Caroline hurried into the bedroom, looking at her phone.

"Hey." Chris grabbed her elbow and drew her to the bathroom door. "What do you think of all the new shelving I built for you?"

Tony narrowed his eyes. "You son of a—"

"It was my idea," Chris reminded him.

Caroline peered around him and gave the space a brief glance. "Oh, it's going to look so great."

"Then why do you have that little frowny line between your eyes?" Jake asked. He rose to his feet.

The line got deeper, and Caroline rubbed at it. She held up her phone. "I got another text from Sam. The tow truck driver still hasn't shown up. She asked if I could check on Maddie and make sure she gets dinner. But I was hoping that you could go check on Sam?" She gave Jake a hopeful look. "It's getting dark out there."

Chris straightened. "What happened? Where's Sam?"

"Her car broke down along the side of Highway 17," Caroline said.

Chris's stomach tensed. He checked his watch. At rush hour that highway was busy. And from personal experience he knew that some people drove like assholes on it.

Chris stepped back as Jake and Tony came out of the bathroom. "Did she say what's wrong with the car?" Jake asked. "Maybe I can bring something to fix—"

"It just stalled," Caroline said. She looked back at her phone. "Look, Sam has been joking with me over text while she waits, but I can read between the lines. She's getting nervous."

Jake pressed a kiss to her forehead. "Don't worry. I'll leave now. Text me her closest exit."

But Chris's legs were already moving towards the bedroom door. "Why don't you guys pick up dinner and head for Maddie? I'll go check on Sam. We can meet back at Sam's apartment."

Tony nodded. "I'll go with princess here. I know more about cars. Maybe I can figure out what's wrong."

Jake nodded. They all spilled outside. "What kind of pizza does Maddie like?" Jake asked Caroline as he held the passenger door to his vehicle open for her.

Tony climbed into the front seat of Chris's F250. His phone buzzed and he held it up. "The two exits Sam is stuck between."

Chris nodded and backed out of the driveway. The engine of his truck growled as he made his way to the highway. He kept the speeding reasonable, but he didn't like the idea of a woman alone on the side of the road.

He didn't like the idea of *Sam* alone on the side of the road.

It took less than ten minutes for them to reach her. Chris's shoulders unbunched when his headlights lit up her figure as he pulled off the highway. They tensed again when he saw the other figure near her. A second car was fifty feet up from their position.

Chris threw the gear into park and hopped out of the truck, Tony following. Something in his chest pinched at the look of relief that crossed Sam's face when she caught sight of him.

"Everything all right here?" Chris asked. He stopped next to Sam and faced the other man. The guy was mid-thirties, his hair was hippie-long, and there was a look in his eye when he stared at Sam that Chris didn't appreciate.

"Fine." Sam laughed lightly but with no real humor. She ran her fingers through the end of her chestnut ponytail. "Stewart here was just staying with me until the tow truck arrived."

"The offer is still good." Stewart sidled closer to Sam. "If you want to sit in my car while we wait."

Chris planted his body in front of Sam's. "Her friends are here now. We got this. Thanks," he added, just in case the guy was actually a Good Samaritan. Some people couldn't help looking creepy.

Stewart's shoulders drooped, but he nodded and left.

Sam blew out a breath.

Chris turned to her. "You okay?"

"Just peachy," she said. She rubbed her arms. "What are you guys doing here? Caroline said you might be coming but I didn't believe it."

Tony snorted. "Do you think Jake would let us leave you out here?"

Chris scowled. "Or that we would want to leave you out here?" What kind of man did she think he was? Or was she so used to doing everything on her own she couldn't recognize a helping hand when it was waving in her face?

Headlights showed a slight flush on her cheeks. "Sorry," she said. "I didn't mean to be rude. It's just... it's been a day."

"No worries." Tony nodded to him. "Should we get her car further down the road, out of the way of traffic?"

"Yep." He pointed his finger at Sam. "Stay here."

Sam narrowed her eyes. He got that familiar zip through his body, the one he felt whenever she turned her snark on him. Or maybe it was those big, brown eyes that were his undoing. "Woof," she said.

He didn't know how she made that woof sound both sarcastic and mocking, but she did. He rolled his eyes then trotted after Tony. During a break in traffic, his friend jumped behind the wheel and Chris circled behind the car. Thankfully, Sam had a tiny piece of shit car that was lightweight and easy to push. They rolled it until the shoulder widened and they had some distance from the highway.

Tony opened the hood and Chris joined him to peer inside. "See anything?"

Pulling a small penlight from his pocket, Tony examined the engine. "Nope. What kind of sound did it make when it stalled?" he asked Sam.

She raised a shoulder. "A spluttering, gagging kind of noise?"

"You have enough gas in the tank?" Chris thought Tony asked the question in the most non-accusatory way possible, but Sam growled.

"I didn't run out of gas. I filled up two days ago."

Tony held up his hand. "Just trying to look for easy solutions. Chris, get in and try to start it. I might be able to see what's wrong then."

Chris climbed in her car, frowned when his knees hit the wheel, and popped the seat back as far as it would go. The key was still in the ignition so he turned it. The engine rumbled to life. He peeked his head out of the window.

Sam's mouth dropped open. "I tried turning the key over and over. It wouldn't start."

Chris climbed out of the car. "It's running smooth as silk now."

"I didn't make my car problems up." Sam crossed her arms over her chest. "It stalled on me."

Tony closed the hood. "Sometimes you get a gremlin playing around. It sounds good now, but we'll follow you home just in case. And you might want to take it to a garage to get it checked."

Sam closed her eyes. The early night cast shadows on her face but couldn't hide her expression. She looked equal parts frustrated and grateful.

A horn blared, and Sam's body jerked.

Chris rubbed his chest. Usually when he saw Sam, she was all smiles and sarcasm. Carefree and happy. But he could see the fatigue wearing her down now.

He didn't like this new Sam. She made him want to do stupid things, like hold her close and take care of her. Things reserved for people in serious relationships.

"Let's get you home," he said, his voice gruff. He guided her to the passenger seat of her car. "I'll drive your car, and Tony will follow in my truck."

"I know how to drive," she said. Her words started out sharp but trailed off into plaintive, like she was trying to maintain the belligerent attitude she had around Chris but was too tired to keep it up.

"I didn't say you couldn't." He pulled the seatbelt around her, clicking it into place. He wasn't going to say he didn't think she was in any shape to drive. There were times it was fun antagonizing the woman, but now wasn't one of them. "I want to listen to the engine as we go. See if I can figure out what made it stop before."

She grumbled, but pulled the door shut and settled in.

Chris tossed his keys to Tony, who nodded. "I'll text Jake," he said. "Tell him to get enough pizza for all of us."

Chris opened the driver's door. "Tell him none of that pineapple crap he likes on top. I want a real pizza."

Tony waved his fingers and headed for the truck.

Another dinner was Sam. Chris shook his head and pulled onto the highway. More time seeing her smile, hearing her laugh. More time arguing with her because he liked to see her get fired up. He was an idiot for subjecting himself to it. He should drop her off and head the hell on home.

But would he? Of course not. Because he was a dumbass.

"I like pineapple on pizza," Sam said.

Chris rolled his head. "Of course, you do." Because why would he and Sam ever agree on anything?

Chapter Five

SAM STUMBLED FROM HER bedroom, yawning. Morning light broke through the large window in her living room. The view of downtown Jacksonville was only somewhat marred by the fire escape she liked to call her red-neck patio.

"Waffles?" she called as she beelined to the open kitchen.

No answer.

Sam frowned at the Starry Night curtain that hid the small laundry nook. She'd never had the extra cash to buy a washing machine or dryer, so when Maddie had moved in, they'd stuffed a single bed in the area and hung the curtain to give her a little privacy.

A breeze ruffled Van Gogh's work, and Sam frowned. She stomped to the living room window and pushed it the remaining two inches shut. She wrinkled her nose at the acrid scent coming through the window. Great. And one of her neighbors had taken up smoking.

She tried to cool her irritation as she headed back to Maddie. Her sister was a teenager. It was hard on both of them sharing a one-bedroom apartment. But Sam indulged in some moments of pure huffiness. Was it too much to ask that Maddie respect her apartment and the things inside?

She flung the curtain back.

Her sister lay on her back, staring at the ceiling. She pulled an ear bud out when she saw Sam. "Yeah?"

"You left the window open last night."

Maddie sat up, swinging her legs around. "No, I didn't."

Sam exhaled for five seconds, inhaled for three. It obviously had to be either her or Maddie, and Sam sure as shit hadn't left it open. But some arguments were best avoided.

"Okay, what do you want for breakfast?" Sam asked, forcing a smile. "It's Saturday, so I was thinking waffles."

Maddie shrugged. "Sure."

Such enthusiasm. First stop in the kitchen, the coffee pot. She got it started and hoped the caffeine jolt would perk her up out of the lousy mood. She pulled a bowl out of the cupboard as Maddie sat at the counter that separated the kitchen from the rest of the apartment.

"What are you up to today?" she asked her sister.

Maddie shrugged again. "Nothing."

"I know Mom would love to see you." Sam hoped that was true. She'd received enough messages from Frank asking for Maddie to come back to visit, but he'd always been the peacekeeper between their mom and them. He might just be saying that because he thought it was what they wanted to hear from their mother.

"I saw her Tuesday. She and Frank came to my game, remember?"

And once a week was enough for Maddie, it seemed. Sam couldn't blame her. A child shouldn't have to see her mother that way. Usually their mom was a nice, sloppy drunk, but she could get ugly on a dime.

"Well, I have an exciting day of errands planned if you want to join me." Sam ladled batter into the waffle iron.

Maddie dipped her chin. "No thanks." She climbed off the stool and went to the fridge, getting orange juice. "So there's a thing tonight." She pulled two glasses from the cupboard and filled them, handing one to Sam.

Sam eyed the glass. Maddie usually became considerate when she wanted something. "A thing?"

"A party," Maddie admitted. "A small one," she hurriedly said. "Bailey and Jaden will be there, along with Aisha and Frederick."

Those were all kids Sam knew, and none of them had been at the party where Maddie had tried drugs. "Where's it going to be?"

"At Aisha's house."

"Are her parents going to be there?"

Maddie rolled her eyes. "Yes, Mom. There will be parental supervision."

Sam smiled tightly. She wasn't Maddie's mom, but that didn't mean she didn't have responsibility. Didn't mean she wouldn't worry. But Maddie had been good this past month. Perhaps she'd earned a bit more freedom and trust. "Okay, but you have to be home by midnight."

Maddie bounced on her toes. "Thanks. Hey, do you have that permission slip I emailed to you?"

Sam groaned. "I left it at work." It's a good thing she wasn't a mom. She kind of sucked at it.

"I need it Monday for that volleyball trip."

Sam rubbed her forehead. "I'll add that to my list of chores today and pick it up."

"Great, and since you're running errands...." Maddie held up a finger then trotted off to her nook. She pulled a plastic supermarket bag from under her bed and tossed it to Sam.

Sam reached for it, but only grabbed the edge. It dropped to the floor, blue fabric spilling out. She bent and picked up a pair of navy boxer-briefs. "What are you doing with these?"

"They're Chris's," Maddie said. "I thought you could give them back to him."

Sam's shoulder blades drew together. "What," she said carefully, "are you doing with Chris's underwear?"

Maddie rolled her eyes. "Chill. It's not like we had crazy monkey-sex in the laundry closet. He got them wet in our bathroom last night after pizza. He asked me for a plastic bag, but didn't want to tell me why. He was embarrassed. It was so cute."

Sam pressed her hand to her abdomen as relief coursed through her. She really didn't want to have to kill Chris. He was a special-forces ninja guy; it would be difficult. Besides, if anyone was going to have crazy monkey-sex with him, it should be—

Nope, not going there. She shoved the underwear back in the bag. "How did he get his underwear wet?"

Maddie held up her hands. "I didn't ask. He didn't tell. You're burning the waffle, btw."

"Crap!" Sam dumped the charred waffle on a plate and tried again.

"How old do you think Chris is?" Maddie slid onto the stool and propped her chin in her hand.

"Too old for you." She didn't know what annoyed her more. Her sister's crush on the man, or the fact that he'd taken off his underwear in her apartment.

The sink in her bathroom was a little touchy. If you turned the faucet lever too far, water spurted out, splashing the person standing in front of it. But why would Chris be standing in only his underwear in her bathroom?

Too many possibilities hurt her brain.

"Age really has nothing to do with maturity levels," Maddie began.

Sam pinned her with a look. "Too. Old. For. You." She tied the handles of the plastic bag into a knot.

Maddie took a sip of her OJ, peering at Sam over the rim of the glass. "I'm not a kid anymore," she said matter-of-factly. "I know what I'm doing."

"You know what you're doing," Sam repeated. Oh God, was her baby sister having sex already? Sam had waited until college before getting horizontal with a boy, but she knew kids were becoming sexualized earlier and earlier these days.

A trend she didn't particularly appreciate and wanted to hide her sister from. But she wanted to keep the channels of communication open between her and Maddie, and she wanted her sister to be safe. It was a fine line to traverse, and Sam hoped she didn't fall flat on her face.

She pasted on a smile that probably looked as fake as it felt. "This might be a good time to talk about safe sex. You really shouldn't have sex"—*ever*—"until you know a person well, until you trust him. But if you do—"

Maddie covered her ears. "Stop. I don't need *the talk*. And I can get condoms at school when I need them."

Sam's heart sank. She really wished Maddie had said *if* she needed them, not when. "Just...please remember my point about waiting until you're serious with someone."

Maddie shook her head. "Don't worry. I'm not sleeping around. Now, instead of sex, can we talk about how you've burned another waffle?"

Sam's gaze darted to the heavy smoke rising from the waffle iron. "Damn it." But inside, Sam was relieved. Sex was really the last thing she wanted to talk to her sister about. She made yet another waffle, but a small pit of unease had opened in her stomach.

Her sister was growing up much too fast, and there wasn't a damn thing she could do to stop it.

Chapter Six

"I'LL BE RIGHT BACK, sweet-ums." Mindy, the cute new waitress at *The Limber Ginger*, gave Chris a flirty wink. She grabbed a tray of drinks from the bar and sauntered off, putting an extra swing into her step.

Chris heaved out a sigh. Aside from her annoying habit of giving the men she served cutesy nicknames (nicknames which, if repeated by any of his squad mates, would justify Chris in ripping out their tongues for calling him them), she was a solid prospect for a good time. Mindy had a good ass, some might even say top tier, but, sadly, it was doing nothing for him tonight. She had brown hair, about the same length as Sam's, but it didn't have that little shimmer of ambers and golds that Sam's did. Her brown eyes didn't have the same sparkle. And her flirtatiousness was too obvious, too easy, when he wanted someone to spar with.

Too easy? Damn, he was fucked up. When had he started craving insults and mockery instead of sweet words? Cleary, he was a masochist.

"What are you smiling about?" Jake leaned his elbows on the bar and waved at the bartender.

Chris forced his lips to flatten. Just thinking about Sam's testy exterior made him happy. But he wasn't going to let Jake, the boyfriend of Sam's best friend, know that. "Nothing." He lowered his voice. "Have you heard anything about future travel plans?"

Jake pointed to his empty beer mug and raised two fingers to the bartender. "Just that Delta squad is on route. If everything goes well, they'll be back next week."

"Do you think we'll be called to assist?" They hadn't been out on a mission in over a month. He was getting itchy. Plus, putting some distance between himself and Sam seemed like a good plan.

"No. Stealth is required, not force. Delta has it."

Chris took a sip of his own beer. Too bad. He liked that part of Africa, too.

The bartender slid two icy glasses in front of Jake.

Jake nodded and turned to go back to their table. It was just him, Tony, and Chris tonight. Caroline was at some work function, and Ryan and Travis had other plans. Chris stood to follow, but Mindy stepped in his way.

"I hope you're not leaving," she said. She set her tray on the bar then leaned her elbows back on it, aiming her breasts at Chris with the precision of a sharpshooter. "I got my fifteen-minute break."

Jake saluted Chris with one of his mugs then threaded his way back across the bar.

"So I was thinking," Mindy said, "since I'm not working tomorrow night that maybe we could—"

Something thwacked into Chris's abdomen.

He grunted and grabbed for the plastic bag before it could make a secondary assault. "What the hell?"

Sam crossed her arms over her chest. She gave Mindy a sweet smile before turning to glare at him. "Your underwear," she said. "You left it at my place last night."

Mindy pushed off the bar. "Asshole," she muttered as she stalked past.

"Nice." Chris drank in the sight of Sam. Jeans that hugged every curve. A T-shirt that stretched delightfully over her assets. Chocolate eyes sparking with irritation. His cock twitched. "She's probably going to spit in my next drink."

Sam stepped to the bar and ordered a Jack and coke. "You were moments away from having your tongue down her throat. What's the difference how you swap your saliva?"

Chris stood behind her, resting one hand on the bar. Heat from her body warmed his front. "Jealous?"

She snorted and looked at him over her shoulder. "Not in a million years." She took a large swallow of her drink.

"Rough day?" Sam was usually a wine or cider kind of girl. Not that he was keeping track of what she liked.

"Just tired." She rolled her shoulders.

Chris gave the bartender a bill. "For her drink and mine."

"No, I got it...." Sam frowned after the bartender, who had smartly taken the money and left. She turned on Chris. Her hip brushed the front of his jeans, and he muffled a groan. "I can buy my own drinks."

"Didn't your mother ever teach you not to turn down a free drink?" he asked.

Sam chuckled harshly. "That is actually one lesson she did try to impart."

Shit. Chris could have kicked himself. He'd forgotten about her mom's drinking problem. "I'm sorry."

Her shoulders drooped. "Don't worry about it. I should really be buying you a drink, to thank you for helping me last night. But since I woke up this morning to find that my baby sister was in possession of your underwear, I'm going to call it even."

The back of Chris's neck went hot. "I wasn't...I didn't...it wasn't like that." There was no way she could think he'd take advantage of Maddie.

"She thinks you two are at the same maturity level. She made a very good argument for why she should be allowed to see you. It almost convinced me not to borrow my momma's shotgun."

Chris's palm slipped on the bar. "Sam, I swear—"

The edges of her eyes crinkled. Her lips twitched.

"Oh." Chris shook his head. "You brat. Somehow, someway, you are going to pay."

She shrugged, not looking a bit remorseful. "Keep your underwear on at my place."

"You need to fix your sink!" And he needed to pull his pants up all the way before washing his hands. Though considering that if he had the front of his pants would have been soaked, something he wouldn't have been able to hide, perhaps it was for the best.

"How's your car?" he asked, hoping to change the subject.

Sam sighed. "It stalled again. Luckily I was already in the parking lot at work. When I came out from my errand, it started right up." She rubbed her forehead. "I'm going to have to take it in to the shop. I don't look forward to that bill."

"Tony is good with cars." The man had restored his 1970 'Cuda by himself. "And I know a bit. Let us take a look. We didn't get much of a chance on the highway."

She held up her hand. "Thanks, but I've got it."

Chris ground his jaw. "You can let people help you, you know? You don't have to do everything yourself."

"I let plenty of people help me." She picked up her drink and stomped around him. "People I trust."

Ouch. He rubbed his chest. How much of that did she mean, and how much was due to the bad habit they'd developed of arguing about everything?

Sam took a couple of steps then stopped, her eyes scanning the room. "Where's Caroline?"

"She's at some work thing." He cupped her elbow and led her toward the guys' table.

"Right. I forgot." She chewed on her bottom lip.

"You're not scared to join us without Caroline as a buffer. Are you?" He nudged her the last couple of feet.

The look she gave him made him worry that her mom might actually have a shotgun she could borrow. Sam was so expressive. Soft and loving when she looked at her sister.

Joyful when she was with Caroline. And around him.... Well, he got all her fire. Anger, irritation, impatience. He liked them all, but he couldn't deny he wouldn't mind seeing some of the softer expressions directed at him, as well.

She greeted Jake and Tony. "Hi, guys. Mind if I join you for one drink?"

Jake pulled out the chair next to him. "Glad to have you."

"It's always welcome having a woman of class and taste join us." Tony saluted her with his drink.

Chris groaned. "Not this again. *The Limber Ginger* is our bar of choice, Viper. Get over it."

Tony scowled. "You know the women I like aren't coming to a place like this. I'm just saying, every once in a while we could go—"

"So, who wants wings?" Chris plucked the menu card from the center of the table and pushed it toward Sam. "The chili lime is pretty damn good," he told her.

"Assholes." Tony tipped back his longneck. He eyed Chris and Sam. "But this night has hope now. How about a dance?" he asked Sam, studiously avoiding Chris's glare. "A two-step is playing. How about it?" He held out his hand.

A smile full of excitement and mischief lit Sam's face. Jealousy churned in Chris's gut. Why didn't she ever look at him that way? And why the hell did he want her to?

Sam placed her drink on the table then reached for Tony's hand.

Chris's body moved on its own. He intercepted her move, enveloping her much smaller hand in his own. "Find your own partner," he told Tony. He tugged Sam to the dance floor.

She stumbled into his chest. Chris wrapped one arm around her waist, locking her body against his, and took her hand. With her height, she fit against him perfectly, like a puzzle piece snapping into place.

"That was rude." She narrowed her eyes but fell into step with the music.

"Yep." He rested his chin near her forehead, inhaling the fruity scent of her shampoo. She smelled like strawberries. "You don't always get what you want being polite."

"And you wanted to dance a two-step?"

He didn't answer. He hadn't cared about the two-step. He'd wanted to get close to her. "I know we hate each other and all, but can we enjoy the dance?" A dance he was an idiot for taking. But when Sam found the right man for her, someone who would be in it for keeps, he wanted to be able to remember moments like these. A few minutes when he was the man who got to hold her.

Her breath gusted across his neck. "I don't hate you, Chris."

He dug his fingertips into her hip. "No?"

She lifted a shoulder. "It's more of a lukewarm dislike." Her teasing voice rolled over him like honey.

"Brat." He tugged her closer.

She didn't resist. Her body melted against his until they felt like one being moving across the floor. It was pure contentment.

Until her phone rang.

Sam leaned back and slid her phone from her pocket. Her feet stopped moving. "It's the police department." A wrinkle creased her forehead as she lifted the phone to her ear. She covered the other one with her palm. "Hello?"

Chris drew her off the dance floor and into the hallway toward the bathrooms, hoping it was quieter.

"Yes, this is Samantha Winters." Her mouth dropped open. She grabbed Chris's arm, her eyes going wide. "What? No. I'll be right there." She shoved her phone back in her pocket. "I have to go."

"What happened?"

Sam dug through her other pockets. "Damn it. Where are my keys?"

Chris gripped her shoulders. "Sam." He waited until she met his gaze. "What happened? What's wrong?"

"It's Maddie." Her voice wavered. "She's been arrested."

Chapter Seven

"WHAT THE HELL WERE you thinking?" Sam twisted in the front of Chris's truck, glaring at her sister who was sprawled in the corner of the back seat.

Mascara streaked Maddie's pale cheeks. Her lips trembled. She looked the epitome of miserable.

Good. "Do you know how badly this could have gone? How having a record could ruin your chances at college?" Sam's heart thudded. Dear God, her baby sister had been one sympathetic cop away from a criminal record. Maddie and three of her friends had all been drinking, and one of them had gotten behind the wheel. Luckily the cop had pulled them over for slow-driving before the idiots could hurt anyone, including themselves.

Chris flexed his fingers around the steering wheel. Ever since they'd left the police station, his jaw had been set and he'd been extremely quiet. Dangerously so.

He'd insisted on driving her to the police station from the bar, and she'd only put up half-hearted resistance. It had been comforting having someone with her to pick up Maddie.

It had been comforting having Chris there.

Sam sighed and rubbed her forehead. She couldn't think about how her very straightforward feelings she'd had about

Chris—irritation, exasperation, and dislike—had morphed into something softer. Oh, he could still get under her skin, but without her knowing it, he'd somehow managed to find his way into her heart, as well.

As a friend. Like how she felt about Jake and the rest of the guys.

"We were just going for iced cream." Maddie placed her fingers on her lips. "*Ice* cream," she enunciated slowly.

Sam closed her eyes. Whatever Chris-sized ball of emotional confusion was swirling around inside of her would have to wait. Her little sister could have ruined her life over friggin' ice cream. That would have to take precedence. "I don't know what's gotten into you these past months, but it's going to stop now," Sam said. "You have your whole life in front of you, and you're not going to destroy it by being a dumbass."

Maddie slumped lower and gazed out the window.

Sam dug her fingers into her thigh. Her sister could have died tonight. Again. Was this a horrible teenage phase, or was there a bigger problem at play? All Sam knew was she didn't feel equipped to handle it.

She should feel lucky. She was just taking her drunk sister back home instead of visiting her in the hospital again. Or planning a funeral. She swiped at the one tear that had managed to escape her eyes.

Scrunched up in the back of the truck, Maddie looked very, very young. Sam's heart softened. "We'll stop and get you something to eat." She took her first full breath since getting that phone call. "That will absorb some of the alcohol and hopefully save you from a raging hangover." In college, when she'd partied a bit too hard, she'd always liked greasy burgers.

Looking at Chris, she said, "Next fast-food place pull over, will you?"

Chris swung his head in her direction. "You want to make her feel better after what she did?" He snorted. "She deserves every second of her hangover tomorrow."

Sam's pulse kicked up. "That's not your call."

He glared into the rearview mirror. "You have some nerve," he said to Maddie, his voice tight. "Not only did you scare your sister half to death, but the moment you and your friends got in that car, you became a deadly weapon. I thought you were smart."

"I am smart." Maddie crossed her arms over her chest. "I used to get straight A's."

Chris huffed. "*Used to* being the operative words. Now you're a dumbass."

"Hey." Sam's skin went hot. The anger almost felt good. This was familiar. Chris overstepping bounds and pushing all her buttons. "Don't talk to my sister that way."

"Someone better tell her how it is. You apparently aren't up to the job."

Sam clenched her fist, her nails digging into her palm. He was such an ass. She couldn't believe her feelings toward him had ever softened. The problem was, she wasn't just angry at Chris. Now it had spread to encompass Maddie for doing something so stupid, and to her mother for being a mess.

And to herself. Mostly to herself. For not handling Maddie right. For letting someone like Chris get under her skin. And for knowing that maybe he was right about her and Maddie.

She'd failed her sister. She didn't know how to be a parent. Sometimes she felt like she could barely take care of herself. Still, if anyone was going to yell at her sister, it was going to be Sam. "Don't talk to my sister that way. It's not your place," she told Chris stiffly.

"No, it's your job." Chris flicked a hard look at her. "You'd better put her in her place pretty damn soon."

"Her place?" Sam twisted so her back was to the door and she could flatten him with her best glare. "What gives you the right to even think that you can tell me what Maddie's place is?"

"I got the right when someone like your sister killed my brother."

Sam shook her head. It was a good thing she was sitting down and strapped in. She blinked until her mind cleared. "Your brother?"

Chris's knuckles went white around the steering wheel. He didn't answer, and Sam wasn't sure she wanted him to. Chris had lost his brother.

Her lungs squeezed, and she looked in the backseat. Maddie's eyes were closed, her mouth hanging slightly open with her soft snores. Sam couldn't imagine what she'd do if she lost Mad. Her mouth opened, but no words came out. She had zero idea what to say to Chris.

And he apparently had nothing more to say to her. The rest of the ride passed in silence. As Chris rolled through her parking lot, Sam saw that her car wasn't back in its place. Tony and Jake hadn't returned it yet. They were probably still having fun at the bar. Why should they cut their evening short just because hers had gone to hell?

She unbuckled her seat belt and reached into the backseat. "Wake up." She shook Maddie's shoulder. "We're home."

"Hate home," Maddie murmured.

Sam shook her harder. "Get up. I'm not carrying you inside." And the way Chris was still glowering, he'd probably sooner dump Maddie on her head or into the dumpster rather than put her to bed.

With a couple more nudges, Maddie was awake enough to stumble out of the truck and toward their apartment. Sam followed behind, ready to catch her if she fell. Chris was two steps behind them. Maddie leaned against Sam during the elevator ride to the third floor.

The smell of alcohol coming off her sister turned Sam's stomach. She was used to seeing her mom like this, but Maddie.... The backs of Sam's eyes burned.

She led her sister down the hall and propped her up near the door as she dug in her purse for her keys. Maddie grabbed the knob, turned it, and staggered into the apartment.

Sam looked from the door to her keys then at the back of Maddie's head. "And you left the apartment unlocked?"

Chris slid past her, grabbed Maddie's shoulders to stop her from going further into the apartment. "Wait here," he said before checking all the rooms. "It doesn't look like anything was taken. You got lucky."

Again seemed to be implied.

"Where's your head at?" she asked Maddie.

"Wasn't me," Maddie mumbled. "I locked it."

Sam dropped her head back and stared at the ceiling. The ceiling wasn't pissing her off right now. The ceiling didn't make her want to scream.

It wasn't worth getting into it with Maddie now. Not when her sister would probably forget this whole conversation anyway. "Go to bed," she told her. She waited until Maddie had disappeared behind her curtain before waving Chris out of the apartment. She followed, and shut the door, making damn sure it was locked.

"Where are you going?" Chris shoved his hands into his pockets.

"For a walk." She strode past him, skipping the elevator and heading for the stairs. "I need to move."

She pressed her lips together when he fell into step beside her on the sidewalk in front of her apartment. "I don't need a lecture right now." She walked faster, but Chris easily kept pace. "I know I'm screwing things up with Maddie. I don't need you pointing it out."

He ran his hand up the back of his head. "Have you called your mom yet? This is her responsibility. Not yours."

Laughter burbled up her throat. Even Sam could hear the hysterical tinge to it. "My mom is probably on her sixth gin and tonic right now. Asking her to discipline Maddie for drinking too much is like asking Mario Andretti to talk to someone about speeding."

Chris blew out a breath. "I'm sorry."

Sam wrapped her arms around her middle. "What are you sorry for? You didn't do anything. I wish...." She sucked in a breath. Ever since she'd received the call from the police station, it had felt like she couldn't fill her lungs. "I wish you could have met Maddie before. She was the sweetest kid, and so responsible."

Chris shrugged out of his jacket and draped it around her shoulders. It was lightweight, but it held the heat from his body, warming her straight through. "She's still sweet. But what do you think changed?"

She shrugged. "Maybe she saw Mom passed out on the couch one too many times. Maybe it's teenage hormones. Who knows?"

The soft snick of their shoes hitting the pavement was the only sound for a while. The moon was three quarters full, and the man up there looked like he was laughing at her. *Asshole*.

Sam stopped at the next corner, staring into the night sky. There was nowhere she could run to that would make this better. Slowly, she turned back. "Will you tell me about your brother?"

Chris's body tensed. He was quiet for so long she didn't think he would answer. A car drove past, its headlights washing over his face. She wished it had remained dark, so she didn't have to see the pain there.

"He was fifteen." Chris's stride shortened. "He and his teammates were coming home from a basketball game. The oldest boy was seventeen, so he was driving. A college student had mixed prescription painkillers with alcohol and T-boned them at an intersection. Paul died instantly."

Sam's stomach churned. She reached for his arm but paused before touching him. She pulled her hand back. "I'm so sorry."

"What are you sorry for?" Chris shot her a sad smile, repeating her words back. "You didn't do anything."

She smacked his arm. It was the only kind of physical contact their love-to-hate-each-other relationship allowed. "Jackass."

"You hit like a girl."

She pressed her lips flat. "I'm trying to be sincere and nice here. It doesn't happen often, so maybe you should appreciate it when it does."

He bumped her shoulder with his own. "I do." His eyebrows drew together. He opened his mouth like he had more to say then snapped it shut. He faced forward again. "What are you going to do about Maddie?"

"Punish her?" Her shoulders sagged. "It's kind of hard to discipline someone when I have no authority, legal or otherwise over her. I could try grounding her until she goes to college?"

"A solid plan," Chris said, "though a bit unimaginative."

"And you have a better idea." Sam arched an eyebrow.

"Boot camp is always a good way to straighten kids out. Adults too."

Sam chuckled. "I'm not sending my sister to the military."

"No, she's not old enough," Chris said slowly. "But I could give her a hell month she won't ever forget." He grinned, the smile looking a tiny bit evil in the moonlight.

"What would that entail?" Sam asked warily.

"Dead sprints on the beach. Push-ups until her arms fell off. Washing all the guys' cars on base. You know, fun things like that."

"You and I have very different ideas of fun." Sam pursed her lips. Still, Maddie needed some type of punishment. And maybe if she was too exhausted physically, she wouldn't have the energy to get into more trouble.

They stopped in front of her apartment building's front door. "I'd like to help get Maddie sorted if I can," Chris said.

She examined his face. He was sincere. He did want to help. "You know, when you're not acting like a jackass, you can actually be kind of sweet."

"Sweet." Chris's voice rose indignantly. "Don't ever tell any of the guys that."

"Your secret is safe with me." *Maybe*. Unless there was an opportunity to give him a hard time. She shrugged out of his jacket and handed it over reluctantly. She already missed being enveloped in his scent. "I'd better be going." But her feet didn't move.

He placed his palm on the wall beside her head. His body shifted closer. "You're doing a good job with Maddie. I don't want you to think otherwise."

"Really?" Good wasn't great, but she'd take any encouragement there was.

He nodded. "She knows that you're in her corner. That's important."

"Thanks." She took a half a step forward, her breasts almost brushing his chest. She ached to lean that little bit farther. "This doesn't mean I'm going to like you all of a sudden."

His toes nudged her shoes. "I wouldn't expect you to make it easy." His voice was a low rumble, like whiskey over rocks. It swirled around her, teasing every place it touched.

"Right back at you." Their gazes locked. The air between them felt heavy, and very, very hot.

This was stupid. She tilted her head as Chris lowered his. This was Chris, the man who drove her nuts and made her want to scream.

Now she wanted him to make her scream in a different way. The sensible part of her brain, the one that knew getting involved with her nemesis would lead to nothing but trouble, kindly sat down and shut up. Sometimes sensible could fuck right off.

She wanted Chris's lips on hers. His hands on her body. She needed it. And after a night like tonight, she damn well deserved it.

His breath ghosted across her mouth. His hand slid down her side and around to cup her butt.

Headlights swung into the parking lot, illuminating them. They both jumped back like guilty kids caught with their hands in the cookie jar. The car parked, and Tony stepped out. He strode toward them.

Sam frowned. "That's not my car." It wasn't Tony's muscle car, either.

Tony bobbed his chin at Chris in the universal male greeting. He turned to Sam. "It's a loaner," he said and handed her the keys. "Your car stalled on me on the way here. I had it towed to a garage my friend owns."

Sam pinched her forehead between her thumb and forefinger. She was starting to feel sick. Her emotions were on a roller coaster ride tonight, and she didn't know if almost kissing Chris was a high point, or a really, effin' stupid point. She did know this was a repair bill she could do without.

"Could this night get any worse?" she muttered.

"Unfortunately, yes." Tony ran a hand through his hair. "At the shop, your car started again. I told my friend about the problems you're having. And even though it's late, he decided to check your car out. He had a suspicion about what was wrong."

"And?" Chris shifted closer to her, as though just his proximity could give her strength.

Maybe it could.

"He found a ping pong ball in your gas tank," Tony said.

Sam gave her head a slight shake. "What? I don't get it. How does a ping pong ball get in my gas tank?"

Chris's nostrils flared. "It gets there when someone puts it there."

Tony nodded. "I'm sorry, Sam, but I think your car was sabotaged."

Chapter Eight

SAM WAVED HER HAND in front of her friend's face, but Caroline's gaze was fixed downward. On the phone she not-so-stealthily held below the table.

"Are you texting Jake?" He was the only person Caroline would ignore the social niceties for, like not looking at her phone while eating breakfast with her best friend.

Caroline's cheeks flushed guiltily. "Of course not." She shoved her phone in her purse. "He just sent me a cat meme."

Sam arched an eyebrow. "Jake. The big, tough Raider. Sent you a cat meme?"

"It was cute." She picked up her glass of ice water and took a sip. "Even Raiders can like cute."

Sam shook her head and filed that information away for later. It would be hella funny if she could plaster his workspace with printed-out cat memes. The rest of the squad would die laughing. She'd probably need Travis to help her get onto base, but he'd be down to help her with the prank. But could it be considered defacing government property if she decorated his desk? She'd hate to face brig time over cat memes.

She stirred sweetener into her ice tea. She'd have to think more on this.

"So how's Maddie doing?" Caroline asked. She cut into her omelet. "Do you think getting arrested has scared her straight?"

Sam's shoulders slumped, all the joy of picturing Jake searching the internet for silly memes for Caroline evaporating. "I don't know. I know kids experiment with stupidity, but I'd thought she'd learned her lesson from the last time. Maybe Chris can get through to her." Though she didn't see how a little physical exercise would have much of an effect if a hospital stay and an arrest didn't get Maddie to clean up her act.

Caroline's forehead wrinkled. "Chris? What's he doing?"

Sam explained his idea of a Maddie boot camp. Caroline laughed until she had to wipe tears from her eyes. "I'm sorry," she said, "but I think Chris is underestimating the power of the teenager. My guess is that Maddie is going to make him more miserable than he'll make her."

"I think you're underestimating him." Sam poked at a strawberry on her plate. "Chris seemed pretty confident he could make a difference." His confidence was one of his most attractive qualities, damn him. What would it have been like if he'd actually kissed her last night? She was both relieved and depressed that Tony had interrupted them.

"*I'm* underestimating Chris." Caroline sat back and leveled her with a stare. "What's going on here? I give you an easy layup to insult the man you profess to loathe, and you defend him instead."

The little scrap of lettuce that her side of fruit rested on drew the ire of her fork next. Why did restaurants think a lettuce leaf would help with their food's presentation? They were usually wilted and sad, like a refugee from a salad bowl.

"Sam?" Caroline dipped her chin.

"Hmm?" She dropped her fork and sighed. "Oh, all right. Chris is obnoxious and overbearing and all of that, but maybe he's not as bad as I thought." She shrugged. "He's good with Maddie, at least."

It was her friend's turn to *hmm*.

"What?" Sam glared at her. "What does that mean?"

Caroline lifted one shoulder. "Nothing. I just find it interesting, is all."

Sam shoveled some French toast into her mouth instead of answering. Nothing she could say would be nice.

The waitress came by and refilled Caroline's coffee cup. Her friend waited for the woman to leave before saying, "This newfound respect for Chris and his abilities, it wouldn't have anything to do with him taking you home the other night?"

It took Sam a moment. "What? No! I didn't sleep with Chris." Although she imagined his abilities in that arena were also worthy of respect. Her belly tingled. God, if he was even half as good as he thought he was, having sex with Chris would be a mind-altering experience.

Caroline finished chewing a bit of egg and cheese. "Then what's with all the Chris-love?"

"It's not Chris-love." Sam sniffed. "It's Chris-grudging-respect."

"Potato, potahto." Caroline jerked her head toward the restaurant's parking lot. "What happened to your car?"

"It's in the shop," she said glumly. "Someone put a ping pong ball in the gas tank. Tony's friend is checking the rest of the car to see if it's been tampered with in any other way."

"What?" Caroline put her fork down. "I don't get it. Why would someone put a ping pong ball in the tank? How did it even fit?"

"I have an older car, and the filler tube is wider. It fit." Sam fiddled with the end of her ponytail. "As to why, I have no idea. When I was driving, the ball would get sucked down to the part of the tank where the gas went to the engine and block it, making my car stall. After the car was stopped for a while, it would float up to the top again, so my car would start. It was really annoying, but nothing inherently dangerous. Probably some asshole kids having fun."

Caroline chewed on her bottom lip. "I don't like it."

"I wasn't a fan, either, but I should have my car back soon." Along with a bill she couldn't afford. She hoped Tony's guy gave friends of a friend discounts.

Her phone rang. She checked the display then silenced the call.

"Someone you don't want to talk to?" Caroline asked.

"My stepdad. He's worried about Maddie." Sam rubbed her forehead. She appreciated Frank's concern, she really did, but he didn't need to call her every day for updates. It just made Sam feel like she was failing when she couldn't give him better news of Maddie.

"He still wants her to move back home?" Sympathy creased Caroline's face.

"Yup." She drained her ice tea. And she didn't know what was the best home for her sister.

What she did know was she was going to be late for work if she didn't get her butt moving. She waved at the waitress and gave the universal sign for 'check please.' "You want to do something this weekend? I was thinking girl-time with just you and Maddie. Maybe a manicure and a movie."

"Sounds like fun. I'll check my schedule." Caroline reached for her purse. "I'd love to discuss this *newfound respect* for Chris some more. Maybe recount all the times I told you he wasn't all that bad while you bitched and moaned about spending time with him."

Sam groaned.

Caroline snapped and pointed her finger at her. "Yeah, just like that."

Sam ground her jaw. 'Girl-time' would now have to include a lot of alcohol if she had any hope of getting through it.

Chapter Nine

"LEFT. LEFT. LEFT, RIGHT, left. I left my wife—"

Maddie cursed. "Your legs are longer than mine," she huffed. "That dumb song doesn't work for me."

Chris didn't lose a step. Maddie had been whining for most of the morning, but she'd also hung in there, doing everything he had, albeit much slower. He and Maddie were jogging along the beach on base on the first of what was to be many days of misery Chris had planned for the little delinquent. He was enjoying the marching songs from basic, but Maddie, it seemed, not so much.

Maddie stumbled to a stop, clutching her side. "I'm dying." She sucked in ragged gulps of air. "I can't do this anymore."

Chris checked his watch as he jogged in place. They'd been running for only ten minutes. Seriously, he didn't know what was wrong with teenagers these days. "If you want a ride home, you'll finish the last mile."

Her eyes narrowed into death-lasers. Maddie had the same eyes as Sam, deep brown with flecks of amber, and quite a few of the same pissy expressions. But where Sam could make a grown man's knees quiver when the full force of her wrath was directed at him, Maddie's snarls just looked adorable. Like a kitten thinking she could take on a bear.

He bit back his grin. "Think what better endurance you'll have for volleyball."

"Ugh." She flipped the end of her ponytail over her shoulder, but she started moving again, so Chris was taking that as a win.

They jogged without speaking. The only sounds were the waves licking the shore, a few gulls in the air, and Maddie wheezing. After a couple minutes, Chris cleared his throat.

"Tell me about living with Sam," he said. "You two getting along?"

"It's... all... right," Maddie gasped out. Her face was turning an alarming shade of red.

"Do you see her a lot?"

Maddie managed to sneer and roll her eyes at him all at once. "Well, duh. We're living together."

"Yes, but...." Christ, it was like he was back in middle school, asking his friend to pass a note to the girl he liked. Women did not affect him this way. He needed to shut the hell up.

His mouth didn't agree. Besides, he had a legitimate reason to ask these questions. One other than his dick wanting to know. "She must go out on a lot of dates, though. Leaving you alone." This was necessary intelligence. If Sam was seeing someone, it would be easier to stop thinking of her in *that* way. His chest tightened. Sam was beautiful and smart. Of course, there'd be a lot of guys circling around her, like sharks to chum.

Though he'd never seen her with anyone. And their near-kiss gave him hope she was single.

No, not hope. He wanted her to be attached. Didn't he?

Maddie laughed. "Nuns get more action than Sam. She's home *every* night, making sure I get my homework done."

The muscles he didn't even realize he'd been clenching relaxed. But that relief was for Sam's sake, he reminded himself, not his. If she wasn't dating someone, that was one less suspect as to who was harassing her.

Chris could only hope it was simple harassment. Making her car stall could be seen as a stupid prank, but it could also have a much darker intention. If Sam's car stopped when she was somewhere isolated, and the asshole was following her....

He clenched his fist. Prank or not, this needed to be shut down. *Now*.

"What about ex-boyfriends?" His voice came out a snarl, and he forced it to soften. "Any that kind of rubbed you the wrong way?"

"Wait. Do you like my sister?" Maddie asked.

"What? No." The back of Chris's neck heated. "I'm concerned whether she's providing a safe environment for you is all." Yeah, good save. Instead of sounding interested in Sam, he sounded like he thought she was fucking up the big-sister gig.

"Uh huh." Maddie's voice rang with disbelief. "Well, it's a good thing for Sam I hate you now. I'd planned on making sure you were so into me you'd never look at another woman again."

It was Chris's turn to stumble. He'd always suspected Maddie had a school-girl crush on him, but her words were too forward for her age, laced with more innuendo than a fifteen-year-old should understand.

"You're a kid." Christ, did all kids talk this way now? "Trust me, I'm not looking at you." No one should be looking at her like that. His scalp prickled. If he could wrap this little one up and send her off to Mayberry, he would.

She snorted. "I'm old enough." Putting on a burst of speed, she raced ahead of him. "Enjoy the view," she shouted over her shoulder.

Chris gaped, his stomach flipping around like a fish in a bucket. Maddie was fifteen going on thirty, and something about that made him very, very uneasy. He appreciated confidence in people, even in kids, but something about Maddie's brand of confidence felt wrong. And he couldn't figure out why.

He easily caught up with her. It was past time to change the subject. He would not be having talks with Sam's sister about why she was too young to be even thinking about certain things. That was definitely a big-sister job. His was to make sure she never thought about drinking and driving again.

"So, back to Sam, someone who's age appropriate for me," he emphasized. "She seeing anyone?"

Maddie shrugged. "There's a guy at work she talks about sometimes, but I don't think she's that into him. Mostly when she talks about work, she talks about the death threats."

Chris blinked. "What threats?" And why the hell hadn't Sam told him about them?

"Against the mayor," she huffed out. She smiled, the first one he'd seen on her face all day. "Someone threatened to sic his pet alligator on the poor guy. Can you imagine?"

Chris's shoulders inched away from his ears. "So these threats are only against the mayor, right? No one's included your sister in any of them?"

Maddie gave him a look. "Of course, they're against the mayor. Why would anyone threaten Sam? She's just a low-level employee."

Chris felt slightly better but it was still something to check out. Along with this guy at work Sam sometimes talked about.

"Thank God," Maddie muttered as his duffel bag and her backpack appeared on the sand. Her phone was ringing, the word Mom lighting up the screen.

"We can take a break if you want to talk to her," Chris said.

Maddie placed her hands on her knees, breathing hard. "No, I'm good."

Chris shifted his weight. "I'm sure she's concerned about you after the other—"

"I'm good," Maddie interrupted, her voice hard. She turned her back on the phone and looked at the ocean while she stretched her quads.

Chris ran his hand through his hair. He was not equipped for this, and that was saying something. In his job, he had to be prepared for everything. He'd faced down thirty insurgents, made innumerable HALO jumps, even had to swim through a piranha-filled river once. But nothing scared him more than facing a moody teenager.

Her mom was falling down on the job, that was clear. Chris had been lucky to have two parents who had their shit together. At least until his brother had died, but he couldn't blame them for falling apart at that point. Are you supposed to survive the loss of a child? He pushed away the disloyal thought that his parents should have held it together for their remaining son. For him. Some losses were just too great.

As much to take Maddie's mind off her mom as it was to take his mind off of his brother, Chris pointed at the sand. "If you're not going to talk to your mom, then it's time for you to drop down and give me fifty."

"Fifty what?"

"Push-ups." He crossed his arms over his chest.

She groaned and flopped to her stomach.

He kept his face expressionless, but inside, his heart smiled. He wasn't usually the ball-buster in the group, but this was fun. He could understand why his Team Chief went home happy every night.

She did one pathetic push up, before scrambling to her knees. "Is that your squad?"

He looked to where she pointed. Jake, Tony, Travis, and Ryan were jogging toward them. Their sweat-slicked T-shirts showed they'd already completed most of their workout, but they'd known what Chris was up to. It appeared they wanted in on the entertainment.

"I guess they decided to finish their PT with us," he said. "How sweet."

"Sweet? What does that even mean?"

Chris's lips twitched. "It means that now the real fun be-gins."

Chapter Ten

SAM LEANED BACK IN her office chair and stared at the ceiling. Her mom's voice droned on like a hive of bees. "I get that mom," she interrupted. "I know, but—"

"It's been five weeks." Her mom sniffed.

"Seven," Frank murmured in the background. "She should be home by now."

"Seven weeks since Maddie's slept in her own bed." The hiss of a can opening sounded through the line.

Beer, or a Coke to mix with Jack Daniels? Sam rubbed her forehead. She shouldn't jump to conclusions. It wasn't even noon. Her mom might just be having a soda water.

The fact Frank needed to give her mother prompts didn't make that charitable thought likely. Nausea swirled through her stomach. She should never have left Maddie alone and gone off to college. She should have taken her out of the house earlier.

"I'll tell Maddie to visit you soon," Sam said, "but I've got plenty of room at my apartment. It's no problem if she stays with me. In fact, it's fun."

Casey stood from his chair a couple desks away and stretched. He ambled in her direction.

"Look, Mom, I've got to get back to work." She kept her voice cheerful. "Maybe we can all have dinner sometime. Okay?" She didn't wait for a response. "Bye," she said and hung up.

"Problems?" Casey asked. He lifted his leg and plopped his left ass cheek onto her desk.

Sam frowned and tugged her memo pad out from underneath his butt. "Family. They're always a problem."

He laughed. "I hear that. Hey, I just went through our messages, and there was one from Helen again." He rolled his eyes. "That woman needs to get a life."

"I like her. And she makes good cookies."

"She's like a one-woman neighborhood watch." Casey pulled out his phone and checked the time.

"I'll call her back after lunch."

"Thank you," Casey said. He smirked. "There are also two messages that only consisted of heavy breathing. I think someone confused us with a phone sex line. Do they still have those?"

Sam gathered her things. Her stomach was rumbling, and an excellent deli was only two blocks away. "Don't know, but it would probably be an easier job than fielding some of the calls we have to." She pulled her purse over her shoulder and started walking.

Casey fell into step beside her. "Going for lunch?"

"Yep." The sun blinded her when she stepped outside, and she dug in her purse for her sunglasses.

"There's a new Indian restaurant on Willow Street." He cleared his throat. "Do you want to get lunch there? Together?"

Sam fiddled with the zipper to her purse. This was the second time he'd asked her out in as many weeks. He was getting more determined, and she didn't know how to let the guy down easy.

"That's really nice of you to ask." Her gaze snagged on a six-foot-something mass of solid muscle leaning against the hood of an F-250. Her shoulders drooped with relief. "But my friend is here." She pointed at Chris and waved enthusiastically. "See you later," she said brightly and trotted down the steps to the parking lot.

Chris's eyes tracked Casey as he slouched to his car. "That guy bothering you?" he asked what she got close.

"No." She drew her eyebrows together. "Why would he be bothering me?"

Chris turned his gaze to meet hers, the beautiful blue of them as hard as sapphires. "Someone messed with your car."

"Well, it wasn't Casey," she said. "He asks me out every so often, but nothing more. He's a nice guy."

"Nice." He crossed his arms over his chest, the muscles beneath his tight T-shirt rippling. "Is that what you want? Nice?"

Sam swallowed back some of her drool. It wasn't fair. His body looked like it was carved from stone, and the way the cotton of his shirt stretched across it should have been a felony. "Everyone wants someone nice. It's not a four-letter word."

He pursed his lips.

"Okay, technically it is a four-letter word, but you know what I meant." She shifted her weight. "What are you doing here?"

He held up his hand, her key ring dangling from one finger. "Your car's been checked out. Tony's friend didn't find any other problems." He nodded to the corner of the lot where her Civic was parked. "Also, I'm hungry," he said. "I have a couple hours before I have to get back to base. I wanted to know if you'd had lunch yet."

Her heart leapt like an insipid school girl's before she tamped down her excitement. This was Chris. And Chris was.... Well, she didn't know what Chris was anymore. A month ago he'd been the scourge of her existence. Now she wondered what his arms would feel like around her. He was confusing, that's what he was.

She didn't like confusing. She grabbed her keys, turned on her heel, and started walking. "I've been craving a Reuben all morning. I'm heading to *Deli Dally*."

He matched her steps. "Sounds good. Tell me about these threats Maddie said your office receives."

Sam squinted at him. "What now?"

"The threats. Any that were directed at you?" His voice was firm. Determined. And Sam felt a bit like she was being interrogated.

"No," she said sharply. "Only the mayor has that privilege, and any legitimate threats that do come through get sent on to the police department. That's what you wanted to talk about?"

"That and other things," Chris said. "Aside from your car, has anything else happened to you lately? Seen anyone following you? Any recent disagreements?"

"No, no, and no." She stopped and planted her hands on her hips. "What is this about? Someone played a trick on me, right? Why are you blowing this up to be a big deal?"

He rested his hands on her shoulders. "It probably isn't a big deal," he said, his voice gentling. "But I want to check it out to be sure. You'll tell me if anything else happens." It wasn't a request.

She hesitated, then jerked her head up and down. She started walking again. It wasn't a bad thing having a special forces guy looking out for her.

"So," he said. "This Casey guy. Have you told him you're not interested?"

"Who says I'm not interested?"

Chris dropped his chin and gave her a look. "Your body language when you were with him screamed it."

She sighed. "I wish he'd pick up on some of that body language."

"You could use, you know, actual language, and just tell him." They hit the sidewalk, and Chris moved to the outside of the pavement.

"Say flat out that I don't think of him in that way?" Sam shook her head. "That's way too harsh." She didn't think of herself as a passive sort of person, but the idea of giving such a pointed rejection made her skin crawl.

"Fine." Chris placed his hand on her lower back and guided her out of the way of a group of teenagers coming toward them. "Say 'I'm sorry' first, then 'I'm not interested.'"

The heat from his palm soaked through her thin blouse. A tiny shiver started at the base of her spine and worked its way up to her neck. "Yeah, that sounds so much better," she said, distracted.

The teenagers passed them, but Chris left his hand where it was. And she didn't tell him to move it.

"Practice on me," he urged. "Tell me you're not interested. Guys aren't good with subtlety. It's better to say things straight out."

"On you it'll be easy." Sam stopped and pushed her sunglasses to the top of her head. She looked him in the eye and pressed one hand to her heart. "Chris, believe me when I tell you, I am utterly and incontrovertibly not..." She made the mistake of meeting his gaze. His deep blue eyes sucked her in, like a whirlpool in the ocean, and she was drowning. "I'm not...."

The air between them heated. He slid his hand around to her hip, that light touch making her breath stall in her lungs. She dropped her eyes down to the hollow of his throat, but even that wasn't safe. When had the space between a man's collarbones become sexy?

She cleared her throat. "Not interested in you." The words came out much breathier than she'd intended. Embarrassingly so.

He grinned devilishly. "Not as easy as you thought, huh?"

She flipped her sunglasses back down, needing to break the connection. She'd thought she'd understood men. Find a decent one, try each other out to see if you could get along for a while, and eventually find someone to settle down with. She liked men, but she was sensible about them. This stomach-churning, butterflies-in-the-throat kind of feeling Chris gave her wasn't in her range of experiences.

She stomped up the sidewalk. She needed to get her head on straight. She had to focus on things like Maddie and paying rent, not how Chris's hair would feel if she ran her hands through it. Or wonder how he'd kiss, soft and exploring or hard and dominant.

They had a good frenemies situation going on, and it was best she stuck to it.

"Maddie was walking very stiffly this morning," she said, eager to change the subject. "She's still sore from your boot camp, and had some very unkind things to say about you." Sam grinned at the memory. At least that little crush was over and done with.

Her smile fell. Only to be replaced with one of her own.

"She's a good kid," Chris said. "But she needs to realize the consequences of her actions."

They reached *Deli Dally*. A line wove out the door and down the sidewalk. Sam and Chris walked to the beginning of it. "You don't seem like the type of guy who's too concerned with consequences," she said.

He lifted a shoulder. "In my job," he said in a low voice, "I think of the consequences to every action. What each act will lead to. We plan for weeks, running through every possible scenario. Our execution has to be faultless."

Sam sobered. She hadn't thought about that side of him. When she saw him, he was always out having a good time. Laughing, teasing, provoking. He must have one hell of a game face when he was sent out on missions.

"In my personal life, it's true I like to have fun." He gave her a sidelong glance. "And I try not to give anyone false impressions about what to expect from me."

They shuffled up in the line, getting closer to the door. Chris was looking very serious all of a sudden, and Sam couldn't handle serious right now. Not from him. She'd had too much of it in other parts of her life.

"Sam, I—"

"My mom wants Maddie to come home." She blurted it out, as much to stop whatever he was going to say as to get his opinion. "Or to be more accurate, Frank, our step-dad, thinks she should come home. After Maddie's latest drinking episode, I can't blame them. What do you think I should do?"

"What do you want to do?" Chris asked.

Sam pondered the question. She wanted Maddie to be happy. Safe. Sam wouldn't mind feeling some security herself. She was out of her depth here.

"I'm scared I'm going to screw everything up with Maddie." She swallowed. "But I want her to stay with me."

Chris nodded. "Let me take you both out some night this week. We have fast-rope training tomorrow, and I'll be wiped out after that, but the night after."

"I don't know." She scored her teeth across her lower lip. She wanted to see him, but maybe more than was sensible.

He placed his hand on her lower back again as they stepped into the deli. It was like he owned that single spot on her. "I have an idea for Maddie. I think it will be good for her."

Then this wouldn't be a date. She could ignore that rolling, fluttery feeling in her stomach that was becoming much too common around Chris. Maybe she was allergic to him. It made as much sense as the alternative.

"Well, if it will help Maddie," she said, doing her best to sound like the martyred, self-sacrificing older sister.

Chris's smirk told her she wasn't as convincing as she'd hoped.

Chapter Eleven

CHRIS PULLED ON HIS blue Henley, the fabric clinging to his still damp skin. He was in the locker room on base, fresh from a shower. He and his squad had trained on the range, and he didn't want to see Sam stinking of GSR.

Jake opened the locker next to him, a towel slung low around his hips. "You almost gave One-Shot a run for his money today."

Chris snorted. His accuracy at distance was improving, but nothing compared to the shots Travis could make. "Maybe I'll get his nickname soon." Travis was already called Skee due to his last name Kowalski. Being the best sniper on the squad had earned him the second nickname.

While Chris still didn't have any.

He blew out a breath. *Whatever.* At least he didn't get a nickname because of something stupid he'd done, like Tony had with Viper.

"I am still, and will always remain, One-Shot to you losers." Travis sauntered into the locker room. He balled up his towel and shot it toward the open bin. "Three points," he said as it landed on top of the other towels.

"You'll get your call sign when you earn one, princess." Jake pulled his clothes from the locker and started changing. "You're seeing Samantha?"

And that's how Jake earned his call sign, Psych. When it came to their personal lives, it could get a bit annoying. Of course, Caroline could have told him about Sam's plans tonight.

Chris checked his reflection in the small mirror at the back of his locker. He smoothed his hair down. "I'm taking her and Maddie to dinner and a field trip."

"A family date?" Jake leaned against the lockers. His light green eyes fixed on Chris, assessing.

Chris's gut clenched at the word family. "Not a date. Only an excursion." A fact he'd had to remind himself of several times. Sam was a friend. Sort of. He wanted to help her and Maddie. He couldn't let this be anything more. Besides, having a teenager along for dinner would have to kill any romantic notions.

"An excursion." Jake crossed his arms over his chest. His voice called bullshit.

And it was BS. Chris wanted more, of course he did, but if they moved on to more, got to the good stuff, then Sam would want things he couldn't give. "We're friends," he said shortly.

"I don't know what I'd call you and Sam." Jake pursed his lips. "Oil and water. Bleach and ammonia. Peanut butter and cheese. Definitely not friends." He closed his locker. "Be careful. And I'm not saying that only because Caroline told me to. You're walking into a delicate situation. I have a feeling it could all go sideways quickly."

Chris grabbed his duffel bag. Jake didn't know the half of it. The guys knew about his brother, but they didn't know how much his death had affected him. That he'd sworn to never have anything the loss of which would destroy him like Paul's death had done to his parents.

"You don't have to worry," he told Jake. "Nothing is going to happen between me and Sam. I've gotta go." He headed for the door. "And peanut butter and cheese are awesome together," he called back. With a nod to his squad, he strode out of the locker room and to the parking lot. Twenty minutes later, he pulled up in front of Sam's apartment. Each of those twenty minutes he used to convince himself that Jake was wrong. That he and Sam were friends.

That friend and her sister were waiting in front of the glass doors to the apartment talking with an older woman in a red track suit. With her white hair and curved shoulders, she looked like she could be anywhere from seventy to a hundred.

He turned off the engine and climbed out of the truck. Sam introduced the woman as one of her neighbors, Helen, and he nodded. "Ma'am."

"It's about time someone courted Samantha," Helen said. "She's a real keeper."

Sam's cheeks flushed red, making her look all kinds of adorable. "Helen, he's not courting, and who even uses that word anymore?"

Maddie snorted. "No one since King Arthur and his knights."

Helen narrowed her eyes. "I'm trying to bring it back. It's a good word." She looked Chris up and down, her mouth puckering. "He looks like he could do a decent job of courting."

Chris grinned. He really shouldn't take as much joy from Sam's discomfort as he did, but she looked as though she wanted the earth to swallow her whole. Something about her being the one off-balance delighted him. Bending at the waist, he gave Helen a mock bow. "Thank you, ma'am. I aim to please."

"We're leaving now." Sam prodded Maddie toward Chris's truck. "Goodnight, Helen."

Chris nodded to the older woman before crossing to Sam. He placed his hand on the passenger door so Sam couldn't open it and waited for Maddie to get in the backseat.

Sam looked from his hand to his face and back again. "Do I need to say the password?"

Smartass. "I would have come up to your apartment to get you. You shouldn't have waited outside."

She waved her hand. "It wasn't a problem. Besides, you're doing us a favor. I didn't want to make you wait."

He stepped closer. Her scent teased him, something sweet and fruity, and it took all his willpower not to lean down and taste her skin. "Let me rephrase that. It's not safe for you to be standing outside waiting. Next time I pick you up for something, you wait inside. Understood?"

Her eyes widened. Tiny flecks of gold swirled in the beautiful chocolate depths. He could read every emotion in those eyes. Irritation that he was telling her what to do. An awareness of his proximity that hit him low in the gut. And a hint of fear over her vulnerability. She hadn't yet accepted that her life had changed, that she needed to take some security precautions, but she was getting there.

Chris hated that she had to worry. He didn't want her looking over her shoulder constantly. Which meant he needed to find whoever had messed with her car. *Fast.* Eliminate the threat from Sam's life.

She nodded, the motion jerky.

He ran his fingers down her ponytail, her hair feeling like silk. He wanted to wind that ponytail around his fist, reel her into him, make her forget that someone was messing with her. Instead, he said, "You're going to be fine." He opened the door for her, waiting until she swung her long, denim clad legs inside, before slamming it shut. He strode around the truck and got behind the wheel.

"I hope you guys aren't too hungry," he said, starting the engine. "My buddy will be going off shift soon, so we're going to stop by and see him first."

"Who's your buddy?" Sam asked the same time Maddie said, "Where are we going?"

"Why don't we let this be a surprise?" Chris pulled onto the street. "What kind of music do you like Maddie?" he asked, turning the radio on.

She glared at him from the backseat. "Whatever." Pulling ear buds from the little backpack she used as a purse, she popped them in her ears and looked out the window.

"Yeah, she's not so happy about this field trip," Sam said.

"Do you care?" Keeping a moody teenager happy wasn't Chris's primary objective.

Sam blew out a breath. "Not if it will help. I still can't believe she got into that car with her friends."

Chris turned the radio to a local country station, keeping the volume low. "Hopefully this excursion will help to scare her straight."

"Where *are* we going?" Sam glanced into the backseat.

"Don't you like surprises?" he teased. Truthfully, he didn't want to give her too much advance notice. Big sis might try to nip this idea in the bud.

"Not unless it involves cake."

"Then this will be good practice for you in building patience." He turned into the city center, heading for the blocks that housed the government buildings.

She growled deep in her throat, making his lips twitch. Sam was altogether too fun to provoke. Which was a good thing, as that was as much fun as he could let their relationship have. He would never know if she was as feisty in bed as she was out of it. Never feel the pleasure of trying to tame her fierceness.

He swallowed, the back of his throat raw. He nodded at a sign as he pulled into a parking lot.

"The morgue?" Sam's voice was shocked. "I'm not sure about this."

"Zeke promised me it wouldn't be gory." He pulled into a spot and cut the engine. "It will show Maddie the real-life consequences of her actions."

They got out of the truck. Maddie pocketed her ear buds and stared with some interest at the sign to the building. "Are we going to see dead bodies?" she asked. "My friends are going to be so jealous."

Chris rolled his neck. He hoped he hadn't made a mistake. "Let's go." He herded them inside. His friend met them at the reception desk. "Thanks for doing this, Zeke." He shook the man's hand and introduced him to Sam and Maddie.

"Not a problem," Zeke said. "Just no one touch anything, okay?"

"What would we want to touch?" Sam asked quietly as Zeke strode down the hallway.

Chris shrugged. Zeke didn't think the way a lot of other people did. Zeke wanted to poke and prod around a morgue. Which was why he worked there.

He nudged Sam forward. Maddie was already hot on Zeke's heels.

They entered a large room, one wall lined with the doors of metal lockers. A large sink and decontamination center were along another wall, and two large silver tables stood in the center of the room.

Zeke whistled as he sauntered to the third locker from the left and pulled the door open. He pulled out the gurney inside. A sheet was draped over a body.

"Cool," Maddie whispered.

Chris gripped his hips. Now he was starting to worry about the kid for a whole other reason. If he had a little Wendy Addams on his hands, this field trip wouldn't do a whole hell of a lot.

"Come on." Zeke waved them forward. "Mr. Garcia might not be going anywhere, but I have to leave in fifteen minutes."

Sam pressed her lips together. She grabbed her sister's arm before the girl could bound up to the table. "Chris...."

"Death is a part of life." Taking her free hand, he led her forward. "It will be okay." He hoped.

They circled the gurney. "I hear you're the young woman who likes to drink and drive." Zeke turned a pleasant smile on Maddie, but his eyes were hard.

"I wasn't the one driving," Maddie muttered.

"Do you really think that matters?" Zeke pulled back the sheet, revealing a middle-aged man with a thinning hairline and prominent nose. There was a bruise on the body's temple and a laceration to the right shoulder. The pucker of the wound was stark against the man's pale skin.

"Mr. Garcia was driving his wife and two boys home when a drunk driver hit him at a busy intersection," Zeke said. "Unfortunately, he didn't die instantly. He had to endure minutes of excruciating pain as fluid filled his lungs. Do you think he cared which snot-nosed kid was behind the wheel of the car that killed him?"

Maddie flinched. Her gaze roamed from the man's head down to the top of the sheet across his chest. Her throat worked as she stared at the body with a defiance Chris could almost respect. "How do you know? Maybe he's happier dead. Maybe his wife and kids were assholes who he was glad to escape."

"Maddie!" Sam said sternly. "Show some respect."

Maddie looked at the toes of her sneakers. "Sorry."

"You have to know what can happen when you behave so irresponsibly." Chris laid his hand on her shoulder. "That could be you on there. It was my brother on there at one time."

Maddie started. "Your brother?" she whispered.

Chris nodded. He'd forgotten the girl had been passed out when he'd told Sam about Paul. "My brother was killed by a drunk driver when he was fifteen." Jesus. Fifteen. The same age Maddie was now. The back of his throat burned, and he swallowed. "So you'll forgive me if I have zero tolerance for bullshit like getting behind the wheel after you've been drinking."

Maddie blinked, her eyes glistening. "Can we go now?"

"Do you understand how destructive, how permanent, your actions could be?" No one could truly understand until it happened to them. The gaping hole that was left when someone you love was torn from your life never fully healed. But he needed Maddie to appreciate the risks she was taking.

She nodded, staring at the floor.

"Then we can go." He nodded to Zeke. "Thanks, man. I owe you one."

"How about a round of pool and a beer." Zeke pulled the sheet up and slid the body back into the locker.

"You got it." Chris herded Sam and Maddie back outside. Everyone was quiet in the truck.

"I don't know about you guys, but I've lost my appetite." Sam propped her elbow on the window frame and rested her head in her hand. "Why don't we just go home?"

Chris drove them back to their apartment, wondering if Maddie had learned anything. There were so many possibilities open to her at that age, equal chances for her to succeed in life or fail horribly. It was frustrating seeing someone fuck up their life. His brother had never had the chance to explore his possibilities.

"I'll walk you up," he said as they parked.

Sam nodded. Her shoulders were drooping, as though she carried the weight of the world. She opened the door to her apartment, waiting for Maddie to slip past before turning to Chris. "Do you want to come inside? I don't know about you, but I could use a drink."

"Sure," he said, a little too eagerly for his liking. This wasn't a date. How many times would he have to tell himself that before he started believing it?

Maddie flopped onto the couch and turned on the TV.

Sam walked around the island and into the kitchen. She pulled two beer bottles from her fridge and a bag of chips from the cupboard. "Follow me," she said, striding past him and to the large window in the living room. She juggled the beer and chips, trying to pull it open.

"Let me." Chris took the food and drink and watched as she crawled through the window onto the fire escape outside. Her jeans clung to the curves of her ass in a way that had Chris stifling a groan. Why couldn't Sam have been a tag chaser, someone happy to flirt, fuck, and forget a military man?

He leaned out the window, placing the bottles and chips down on the serrated metal before hauling himself through. He closed the window behind him, muffling the sounds of the TV. "Uh, you come out here often?"

"It's my redneck patio." Sam leaned against the rail and placed her beer on the step leading up to the next floor. "Fresh air and sun, or moonlight, as the case may be. What more could a girl ask for?"

Chris sat with his legs stretching onto the stairs leading down. "I like that you make the best of things."

"I try to." She looked through the window at Maddie. "I don't always succeed."

Chris twisted the cap off his beer, waited for Sam to do the same, then tapped the neck of his bottle against hers. "Always faithful. Always forward."

She arched an eyebrow.

"The Raiders' motto. It felt fitting." He shrugged.

Sam opened the chips. "Do you think seeing Mr. Garcia helped Maddie? It seemed like it shook her up a bit. In a good way."

"I hope so." He tipped his bottle back and took a swallow. "But I have to admit poor Mr. Garcia wasn't actually a victim of drunk driving. He fell off his roof cleaning his gutters."

"What?" Sam threw a chip at him. "You got me to a morgue under false pretenses."

"This town isn't big enough to have a body in the morgue at all times due to drinking and driving. Thank God." He picked the chip off his chest and popped it in his mouth. "But if it makes you feel better, there was a woman there last week who'd killed herself driving into a brick wall while high."

"Yeah," Sam said sarcastically. "That makes me feel great."

Chris grinned. He grabbed the bag of chips. "I do whatever it takes to get the job done."

"I bet." She took a slug of beer, eyeing him over the bottle. "I'm not sure I like seeing this side of you."

"What side is that?"

"The helpful, non-douchy side."

"Thanks. I think."

Sam ran her thumb over the lip of the bottle. "You went from the annoying friend of Caroline's boyfriend to...."

His pulse kicked up. "To what? And I'm Caroline's friend, too." He and the rest of the guys had helped rescue her from a shit-stain drug dealer a couple months ago. He should damn well hope that raised a man above acquaintance category.

Sam rolled her eyes, the light from the living room casting a golden glow across her face. He used to think that Sam was cute. Cute and hot, especially when she wore shorts or a skirt, showing off those long, toned legs. But she was more than that. She was beautiful. Someone he could stare out for ages and never get bored.

He held the chips out to her, and when she reached for it, he grabbed her hand and pulled her close. "What am I now?" he asked in a low voice.

Her breaths grew short. Her gaze flicked from his eyes to his mouth and back again. "Honestly, I have no idea."

"What do you want me to be?" He could be a lot for her. A man who made her smile. Made her scream. His cock pressed against his zipper and he resisted the urge to press his palm against his hard-on. There was only one thing he wouldn't be.

"I...." Sam scraped her teeth over her bottom lip. "Oh, hell." She rolled onto her hip. Her breast plumped against his arm, making him throb. Grasping the back of his head, she dragged him down and took his mouth.

Chris pressed a hand to the back of her neck, the other her hip, and pulled her tight to his body. He slid his tongue inside her mouth, salt, and hops, and Sam's unique flavor exploding on his taste buds. He slanted his head, took it deeper until he felt like he could devour her.

Sam mewled. She rested her palm on his abdomen. Blazed a path south, detouring around the bulge in his pants and stroking his inner thigh. So damn close to where he needed her touch.

His teeth scored her throat as he figured out the logistics. They were in public, but it was dark. Maddie could look out the window at any moment. Could they sneak into Sam's room without Maddie knowing he was going to fuck her sister like a rabbit in heat?

He inched his hand under her top and found her breast. The swell was big enough to fill his palm, and her nipple puckered behind the lace of her bra. He circled his thumb around the peak until Sam moaned and arched into him.

His truck. They could find some privacy in his truck. But first, he needed to be straight with her. There was no way he'd be accused of taking advantage of Sam.

He pulled back. Sam's eyes had sunk to half-mast. Her lips were red and glistening, tempting him to go back in for another taste. Her gorgeous chest rose and fell, her breast pressing into his hand. "Sam, I want to be honest with you."

She blinked, her unfocused eyes going sharp. She shifted away from him. "Oh boy. Nothing good ever comes from that start."

He pressed his fists into his thigh. His skin itched to hold her again. "You have to know I'm insanely attracted to you. I mean, most of our fights are basically foreplay."

She opened her mouth, probably to deny it, tell him he was full of shit, but he pressed on. "And I'd love nothing more than a casual relationship with you. But you have to know that I don't do serious. Maybe if I find a woman who feels the way I do, that will change, but I haven't met her yet."

Her forehead wrinkled. "You'll get serious with a woman who feels the way you do about not wanting a serious relationship?"

He huffed out a laugh. "No. I don't want kids, Sam. And most women see that as a deal-breaker for a serious relationship."

"Whoa." Sam held up a hand. She scuttled further away. "Why are you talking about kids? Who talks about kids already? That conversation is at least a date five topic, and we haven't even decided if we like each other enough to go on date one."

"We've been circling each other like dogs in heat ever since we met." He placed his palm on the floor of the fire escape. He frowned, looking down at what his fingers had brushed.

"Okay, this night's over." Sam stood and brushed the seat of her jeans. "Kids," she muttered. She bent and grabbed the bag of chips. "This is getting too weird, and it's already been an intense night. I just want to watch a mindless popcorn flick and go to bed. What I don't need is to think about getting into a frenemy-with-benefits relationship now. With how tired I am, I would definitely make the wrong decision."

His mind wanted to explore the possibilities that 'benefits' entailed, but now wasn't the time. He put his hand on her leg before she could leave. He held up the cigarette butt that had been discarded on the fire escape. "You think Maddie's smoking?"

Sam's lips pressed tight. "No. One of my neighbors, I guess." Her forehead furrowed. "There's a whole pile of butts in that corner." She pointed. "Like someone was sitting here and...." She stared through the window into the living room. "Oh, God. Why do I hope it was Maddie smoking?"

A pile of cigarette butts didn't have to mean anything. It could have been some kid on another floor who wanted to smoke away from his mom's eye.

But it could also mean something.

Sam took deep breaths before pushing the window open. She crawled over his legs into the apartment.

He followed, draining his beer. The lock on the window was a flimsy piece of shit, but it was better than nothing. He drew the curtain closed. "Sam—"

"Thanks for tonight," she said brightly, shooting a look at Maddie. "We appreciate it."

Chris raked his hand through his hair. He hated this. Everything was too vague. He almost wished an overt threat had been made. Then he'd know where they stood, know what actions to take. As it was, Sam could be victim of nothing more than pranks and coincidences.

Nodding, he said goodnight to Maddie and Sam, and left her apartment. He waited to hear the deadbolt slide closed before heading for the elevator. When he got outside, he circled around her building until he stood underneath Sam's window.

The ladder to the fire escape was above him. He jumped once, twice. The third time, the tips of his fingers gripped the bottom rung. The ladder slid down noiselessly as he fell back to earth.

Chris moved the ladder up and down. He'd never seen a fire escape ladder so well-maintained. Almost like it had been recently oiled.

His phone rang. He pushed the ladder back up as he answered. "Yeah."

"Get to base," Jake said.

Chris's stomach sank. There was only one reason to head in at this time of day. He looked at the fire escape. He had a bad feeling the cigarettes were related to whoever was harassing Sam. He didn't want to leave town, not now.

With little hope, he asked, "What's up?" Please let it just be a briefing.

"We're wheels up in five."

Son of a bitch.

Chapter Twelve

"MADDIE!" SAM SHOOK HER sister's shoulder. "You're late for boot camp."

Her sister rolled over in her narrow bed and gave Sam her back. "Cancelled."

Sam wrapped her robe around her. It was getting chilly in the mornings. Pretty soon she'd have to turn the heat on. "What do you mean 'cancelled?' Who cancelled it?"

"Chris." Maddie flipped to her back and yawned. "Texted me late last night. Said it was off for a couple of days. He'd let me know when we'd start again. Yippee." She swirled a finger in the air.

"Huh." She'd have thought Chris would have mentioned that to her when they'd had their little heart-to-heart on the fire escape last night. Maybe he'd been as anxious to leave as she'd been. It wasn't every day that the guy you despised but really sort of lusted after tells you that he doesn't do relationships but hey, how about some good, hard fucking?

Her stomach tingled. Okay, he hadn't said the good, hard fucking bit. That was just how she imagined they'd be together. And she was here for it. If she could wrap her head around the idea of a no-strings, expiration-date-stamped relationship.

"Are you going to just stare at me?" Maddie frowned. "It's creepy."

Sam blinked. "I wasn't...I was just thinking." About how Chris would feel between her thighs. Her cheeks heated. "Do you want to sleep another hour before school?"

Her sister gave her the gimlet eye. "It's Saturday."

"Oh." *Right.* She blew out a breath, her lips vibrating. Which meant brunch with Caroline, something fun, but she needed to clear her head beforehand. "I'm going for a jog. Want to join?"

Maddie groaned and pulled her comforter over her face.

A no, then. Sam got ready and headed out the door. By the time she got back from her run, she was fully awake and looking forward to the weekend.

"Do you want to join me and Caroline?" she asked her sister after her shower.

"No, thanks." Maddie pulled a bowl and a box of cereal down from the kitchen cupboards. "Can I hang with Bailey today?"

Sam put her earrings in. "She can come here. You can go to the beach, the mall, or the movies. No parties."

Maddie nodded.

Sam hesitated at the door. "Make sure you lock up and keep the curtains closed." She couldn't imagine anyone perving at them from the fire escape in broad daylight, but still, she felt uneasy.

"Why?"

"We might have a peeping Tom." Sam shifted her weight. She didn't want to scare her sister but she needed her to be careful.

Maddie dropped her spoon, milk splashing onto the counter. "What?"

"It looks like someone's been sitting on our patio." She waved at the curtain-covered living room window. "It could just be another resident escaping their apartment for a bit, but better to be safe than sorry."

"Is it the person who messed with your car?" Maddie gripped the counter, her knuckles going white. "Do you know who it is?"

"I don't know." Sam tilted her head. She'd thought her sister would shrug this off, make fun of her for being worried. Uneasiness swirled through her stomach. "Do you know who's doing this?"

"I..." Maddie opened her mouth, closed it. Opened it again. "Sam. I think... I mean, I need to...." Her shoulders rounded, and she stared down into her bowl. "No, I don't know."

Sam ground her jaw. Why wouldn't her sister open up to her? If she was scared, Sam wanted to know. She could help her through it. She'd be there for any problem her sister had. She wanted to demand answers but knew from past experience how well that would go. Maddie was an expert at shutting down and shutting her out.

"Okay, I'll see you later." Sam slid her purse strap on her shoulder. "Tacos tonight. Ask Bailey if she wants to stay for dinner."

Maddie didn't answer.

Sam made sure the door was locked when she left. She leaned her forehead against it, all the endorphins from her jog gone. She hoped Caroline could bring back some of her happy.

Her friend was up to the job. "I have two gift cards for massages and mani/pedis at the Jasmine Spa. What do you say we try to squeeze ourselves into their schedule today?"

Sam picked up a slice of bacon and took a bite. She did a little food-dance in her chair. Bacon could solve most any problem. "How did you get those?"

"Jake." Caroline flipped the end of her pale-blond ponytail over her shoulder, looking smug. "He lost a bet that I couldn't get into a...uh... yoga pose."

Sam looked at her friend steadily as she chewed. "It was a sex position, wasn't it?"

Caroline flushed. "Not important. What is important is that we both deserve hot masseurs massaging away all our tensions." She grimaced. "Mine will have to be a hot lady masseuse. I promised Jake before he left."

Sam snorted. Massage therapists were professionals, but she could well believe Jake wouldn't want another man touching Caroline. No man had ever been so possessive of her friend. Sam was a bit jealous. No man had ever cared enough to be possessive over her.

She cut into her eggs benedict, the yolk oozing over the puff pastry. "So the guys." She looked around to make sure no one was listening. "They're away?"

"Yes." Caroline stabbed at her breakfast burrito. "I'm trying to be a good military girlfriend, but this part sucks."

At least Jake told Caroline he was leaving. Chris hadn't even bothered telling her. Not that she was his girlfriend. Sam didn't deserve the same considerations, but being left out of the loop still hurt.

After all the fights, the snark, the dirty looks, she wanted something more with Chris now. And she wasn't sure she should want that.

"So, Chris." She turned her fork around in her fingers. "You like him, right?"

Caroline sat back in her chair, a smirk dancing around her lips. "Not as much as you like him."

Sam threw her straw wrapper at Caroline. "He doesn't want anything permanent, but he is interested in a frenemy-with-benefits relationship."

"Frenemy-with benefits? That's too wordy." Caroline tapped her finger against her lips. "What about fuckemy?"

"I don't care about the terminology." She huffed, her lips twitching. "I care about whether it's a good idea or not."

"Why doesn't he want a relationship?" Caroline frowned. "What's wrong with him?"

Sam pushed her plate away. "I don't know. Something about not wanting kids." She still couldn't believe he'd brought up children when she'd been five seconds away from riding his thigh like a bull. Who did that?

All she'd wanted was something physical.

Just hot, sweaty sex.

She hadn't been thinking about commitment.

But would she have wanted one after? She wasn't usually a one-night-stand kind of woman. Maybe Chris had been right to give her a warning.

"I don't think it's unusual for men in that career to feel that way." Caroline tapped her fork against her lips. "Some guys with dangerous jobs don't want the whole wife and kids thing. They don't want anyone to mourn them if they don't come back." She swallowed, her face going dark.

"That's not going to happen to Jake," Sam said firmly.

"Of course not." Her friend smiled, but it was as weak as herbal tea. "Back to you. Can you deal with a fuckemy situation?"

Sam scowled. "We're not calling it that. And I don't know."

The waitress came with their bill, and Sam put cash on the table.

She and Caroline made their way out of the restaurant. "Mad and I are having tacos tonight if you want to join us."

"I might." Caroline sighed. "The house feels empty without Jake there."

"Then get your ass to my place. We can watch a moo...vie." Sam stopped. Her car was parked under a magnolia tree in the corner of the restaurant's lot. Petals had drifted down to decorate the Honda Civic. The image would have been lovely...except for the word *Bitch* keyed into her driver's side door.

Caroline cursed. "I don't like this, Sam. We can't ignore it anymore. Someone has it out for you."

Sam's chest felt tight, like a vise had her in its grip. No, there was no pretending this was random any longer. No one had ever hated her before. It was an odd feeling, like the animosity was a physical being, reaching for her. Especially since she had no idea who she'd pissed off.

"I wish Jake was home." Caroline rubbed her forehead. "He'd know what to do about this."

Sam prided herself on being an independent problem-solver herself, but she had to admit she wished Chris was there, as well. Someone to help share her burden. Someone she trusted to keep her safe.

But Chris wasn't there. She had to deal with her problems on her own, like always.

She pulled her phone from her purse and pulled up the number to the police department. Her life was such a disaster she had the number in her contacts now.

She turned her back on her car and made the call.

Chapter Thirteen

PSYCH HELD UP HIS gloved hand. Three fingers. Two. One.

Travis kicked in the flimsy door, and they made entry. The lights attached to the barrels of their MK 18s swept the dusty interior. Two insurgents jumped from their chairs before hitting the floor, lifeless.

The squat structure was like every other home in the village. Run down. Squalid. Thirty miles from N'Djamena, this outpost was known as the thieves' den of Chad.

Chris followed Tony down the narrow hall. Shouts emerged from the back room, one man barreling out, waving his handgun.

Tony took him out with two shots.

Chris stepped into the room. The windows were covered with sheets. Their target sat on a wooden chair, arms tied behind his back, a pillowcase over his head.

Another man stood behind him, holding a pistol to the man's head. "I kill him. I—"

Chris squeezed his trigger. He went to where the man dropped and kicked his weapon away from his limp hand. Pulling his Ka-Bar from his belt, he cut away their target's bonds. He hauled the guy to his feet. "Let's go."

The guy stumbled and reached for the pillowcase.

"Leave it." Chris followed Tony back down the hall, gripping the man's arm firmly. They didn't have time to deal with the guy's eyes adjusting to the light. That, and the dude was an asshole. Just because the US government thought he would make a good asset didn't make him a good guy.

For the first time in his career, he hated his mission. Instead of being at home and helping Sam, he was across the globe rescuing an arms' dealer who had more blood on his hands than Jack the Ripper. He'd asked some friends in Delta squad to keep an eye on her, but it wasn't the same.

A woman's scream ripped through the night, quickly silenced. Outside the front door, Jake held a local woman tight to his body, his hand covering her mouth. He jerked his chin at Chris.

Handing his package off to Travis, he rested his hand on the woman's shoulder and spoke to her in a low voice. He was the only one in his squad who spoke decent Arabic.

Tony picked up a bag at the woman's feet. "Food delivery," he said.

Chris nodded, and kept speaking to her in a soothing tone. "Go home," he told her. "There's no one here to take delivery. You understand?"

Her gaze jumped from each member of the team, landing on the Humvee as Ryan drove up. She jerked her head up and down.

"Let's go," Jake said.

Travis already had their target in the vehicle, and the rest of the men quickly followed. The woman scampered away into the dark.

Jake checked his watch. "Wheels up in fifteen."

"Think you can get us there without hitting every pothole this time?" Tony asked Ryan.

"Please." The word was muffled behind the pillowcase, and heavily accented. "Please."

Jake pulled the case from his head. "You are now under the protection of the United States government. We received your message. You're heading to America."

The man closed his eyes, muttering 'Thank God' in his own language. He lightly pressed his fingers to the bruised skin around his eye. "Could you not have picked me up before I was taken?"

Chris stared out the window. The asset had spent his life making money off of others' suffering, until he'd screwed the wrong client. It was only when he knew there was a target on his back that he'd approached a contact in the U.S. government. With the man's knowledge of warlords and cartel leaders, Uncle Sam was plenty eager to pick him up. Offer him a new life, courtesy of the American taxpayer.

Chris clenched the barrel of his rifle. He didn't want to be here. Didn't want to protect the scum of the earth while Sam was vulnerable. Sweat beaded on the back of his neck. He liked to think that America was safer than the rest of the world, and realistically, he knew it was. But shit still happened, even in Jacksonville, North Carolina. The attacks on Caroline after her run in with a drug dealer were proof of that.

He forced his breathing to stay even. He should have asked Delta for 24-hour surveillance over Sam. Maybe asked one of them to stay with her and Maddie. As it was, their drive-bys and monitoring of emergency calls was less than adequate, not if someone really wanted to hurt Sam. But he hadn't thought there was enough evidence to justify asking for full protection.

He'd been an idiot. He should have listened to his gut. Someone was targeting her, and he was in Africa saving an arms' dealer.

They rolled onto the airport grounds. Ryan drove onto the tarmac, pulling up next to a C130. They formed a tight circle around their target and hustled him up the cargo door and into the plane.

In sixteen hours Chris would be stateside. Sixteen hours to kick himself for being a fool. Sixteen hours to pray nothing had happened to Sam.

Their target strapped himself into a seat. "I asked for your help four days ago. If you had come immediately, I wouldn't have been taken."

Jake slapped him on the shoulder. Hard. The man jerked forward. "Just be glad we weren't a day later."

Tony handed the asshole a bottle of water and asked about other injuries.

Chris stalked to the front of the hold, needing distance from everyone. In their line of work, a day could mean life and death.

He exhaled, his breath coming out in jagged huffs.

He could only hope he wasn't a day too late for Sam.

Chapter
Fourteen

A PHONE BUZZED. SAM buried her head under her pillow, but the sound still snuck through. "Shut it up," she mumbled.

A foot kicked her leg.

"Ow." Sam tossed the comforter back and rubbed her calf. "You suck as a bed partner."

Caroline blinked blearily at her, before rolling over and reaching for her cell on the nightstand. "It's Jake." She sat up, much more alert. "He's back."

"Good. Then I don't have to sleep with you anymore." Sam yawned. Caroline had spent the night at her apartment the past two days. She'd told Sam it was because she didn't like being alone when Jake was gone, but Sam knew her friend was worried about her after the car incident. Which was sweet, but Sam didn't have a guest bedroom and Caroline said her couch was too lumpy.

Which left them cozying it up together in Sam's bed. Not the person Sam wanted to be snuggling up to.

She picked up her own phone and looked at the time. "It's five a.m." She glared at Caroline. "No one should be texting at five a.m."

Caroline sent a reply, then rolled out of bed and started dragging on a pair of jeans. "He just got home. He wanted to know, and I quote, 'Where the hell is your sexy ass? I get home and my woman is AWOL?'" She grinned. "I want to see him before I go to work."

"And by see him, you mean his peen?"

Caroline whacked her with her shirt before tugging it on.

Sam sat up, scooting back so she could lean against the headboard. "So he's okay? They're all okay?" She tried to sound casual, like she was just generally concerned about all of Jake's friends.

Her friend gave her a knowing look. "They're fine. If something had gone sideways, he wouldn't have led with 'sexy ass.'"

Sam rubbed her sternum. Caroline was so happy she nearly glowed. Hearing from her boyfriend had made her practically blissful, and no one should be blissful at five a.m. Sam was happy for her bestie. She wanted everything roses, cotton candy, and unicorns for her friend. But seeing Caroline light up from only a text made Sam realize how much she was missing in her life.

She hadn't had a steady boyfriend since college, and even then it hadn't been that serious. There had been no talk about seeing each other after he went back home to Raleigh. They hadn't shared their biggest desires, their secrets or dreams. It had been a relationship of convenience. Sam had never looked at a man the way Caroline did Jake.

And now the man she thought she might want to get close to, the man she wanted texting her when he arrived home safe, told her he didn't do serious.

She blew her cheeks out then let the air out with a hiss. Maybe she could go back to hating Chris. Start a big fight with him. Go back to the way things were.

Caroline grabbed her purse. She paused at the bedroom door. "You'll be okay?"

Sam forced a smile. "Go. Get yourself some lovin' before work. Start the week off right."

"It's the only way to handle Monday mornings," Caroline agreed. "I'll call you later."

Sam trailed in the path her friend had made, locking the front door behind Caroline. She leaned against it and studied her apartment. It was dark, a blessing as there was no reminder that she had skipped vacuuming for the past two weeks. She plodded across the for-sure dirty carpet and stood in front of the curtains of the living room window.

She wrapped her fingers around the edge of a curtain, held her breath, and whipped it back. Her body sagged. The fire escape was empty. Dawn was slowly breaking, the world outside a dull gray. She released the curtain, watching it flutter back into place.

She returned to her bed and rolled onto the mattress. Should she try to go back to sleep? She'd have to get up again in less than an hour, but the thought of trying to do something productive with her extra time made her wrinkle her nose.

She picked up her phone. Put it down. If Jake was home, so was Chris. It would only be polite to check in on him. He couldn't tell her anything about his trip, but knowing someone cared whether he made it back in one piece would have to bring him a smile.

God, she was full of shit. She wanted the connection for herself. It was too early in the morning for good judgment. She picked up her phone and texted him. *You got back okay?*

A moment later, her phone rang.

"Hi," she answered breathily. She cleared her throat. "I was with Caroline when Jake got back."

"I wanted to call when I landed." His voice rumbled through her body. It flustered her the same time it warmed her straight through. "I didn't think you'd be awake yet. How have you been?"

He wasn't asking the question generally. He didn't care about the mood she was in, or what she'd done while he was gone, the normal things a boyfriend might want to know after he'd been gone on a trip. He wanted to know if there had been any other incidents.

Her shoulders curled. "I'm fine."

A pause. "There's fine, and then there's *fine*. Which kind are you?"

"Whichever kind means the same as when you left." The kind that meant she was still as screwed up as ever.

"I want to see you. Determine for myself just how fine you are," Chris said. "Meet me for breakfast."

"Is that a request or an order?"

She could hear the smile in his voice. "Whichever gets your ass out of bed and out to breakfast with me."

Sam bobbed her heels on the mattress. She didn't want to be, but she was excited to see him. "Somewhere close to City Hall?"

He named a diner and they hung up.

Chris wanted to discuss her problems.

She wanted him.

She was tired of denying the truth to herself. Tired of fighting the attraction.

She went to her closet to find the sexiest, but still work-appropriate, outfit she owned. And maybe if she turned his head enough, Chris would forget all about his no-strings rule.

Sam's car was parked on the street in front of the diner. Chris parked across the street and jogged across. He frowned. There was a fresh paint job on her driver's door, the blue not an exact match to the rest of the car.

He hurried into the restaurant, scanned the interior. Sam was in a booth near the back. She wore some sort of lacy tank top, the tiny straps exposing the smooth skin of her shoulders. A business jacket rested on her purse by her side.

Chris yanked his gaze up to her face as he sat across from her. He wouldn't be distracted. "What happened to your car?"

"Well, hello to you, too." Sam leaned forward, resting her elbows on the table. The vee of her top dipped, exposing alluring shadows.

"Your car," Chris gritted out. He wanted to drink in the sight of her, let his gaze roam every curve, but he'd spent the past thirty-six hours worried sick over her safety. He needed a sitrep. Now.

"My car's fine." She waved her fingers. "I've been more concerned about you." Her eyes roamed his body, examining every inch she could see. The small wrinkle in her forehead smoothed. "No injuries."

Chris swallowed. He felt his heart beat, slowly, deeply. No woman had ever looked so relieved to see him. Like while he'd been worrying over her, she'd lost sleep over his safety. He didn't want her, or anyone worrying about him, but he had to admit, it felt... nice.

"Please tell me what happened to your car." He rested his hand atop hers.

She looked into her mug of coffee. "Someone keyed it. Scratched the word *Bitch* on the door. I was lucky the body shop could get me in so quickly to paint over it."

Rage coursed through his veins, making every muscle in his body tense. He kept his hand on hers gentle, however. "I want—"

"What can I get you two?" A waitress stood next to the table. She held up a pot of coffee, and Chris flipped his mug over for her to pour.

Sam sat back, sliding her hands into her lap. His palm felt empty without her skin beneath it. They ordered and waited for the waitress to leave.

"I want you and Maddie to come stay with me," he said. "I'll try to resolve this situation as quickly as possible, but I don't feel comfortable with you two alone."

Sam blinked. "We can't do that. Maddie has school. I have work."

"And you can still go, you'll just leave from my place." He should have thought of this before. Sam's apartment was too vulnerable. It would be easy enough to break the window into her living room. She and Maddie would be sitting ducks.

Sam rubbed her thumb along the rim of her mug. "I don't want to upset Maddie more than she is. Moving on top of finding out I'm being harassed...."

"She'll be a lot more upset if something happens to her sister," Chris growled. His gut twisted. He wouldn't let that happen. "I have a four-bedroom house. There's plenty of room."

"Why do you have such a big house?" She tilted her head. "Were you married?"

"No."

The waitress returned and slid their plates onto the table. "Enjoy," she said.

Chris picked up his fork. Instead of eating, he turned the implement around in his fingers. Married. It was a rational question. His fingers were as cold as the metal they held. This was the perfect opportunity to lay his cards on the table. He needed Sam to know what she was getting into with him, *if* she wanted to get into anything.

"I don't ever intend to be," he said in a low voice.

"What?" Sam paused, a bite of pancake midway to her mouth.

"Married. You asked about that." He sat back and rubbed the back of his neck. "When I told you I wasn't looking for anything serious, I meant it."

She carefully placed her fork down. "Do you want to talk about why?"

He really didn't. But Sam deserved to hear it. "I already told you about my brother."

She nodded.

"I didn't tell you about how his death destroyed our family." He took a sip of coffee. "My parents were never the same. Home life was full of fighting, drinking. They divorced eventually, but not before they'd broken each other even more."

"And you?" Sam's velvety eyes held steady on his face.

He gripped the edge of the table. "I think it hurt them to look at me. Paul and I looked a lot alike. I was mostly ignored." He would have preferred if they'd screamed at him, too. Even thrown things. Made him feel something other than invisible. His heart clenched. There had been times when he'd wondered if he'd died alongside his brother.

"I'm sorry your parents weren't there for you." Sam rested her forearms on the table. "But we're all going to die, Chris. It's how you live your life that—"

"No." He chuckled, but it was harsh, bitter. "That saying, that it's better to have loved and lost than never to have loved at all? It's bullshit. There are some things you don't recover from. The loss of a child is one of those. I won't put myself through it."

"And that's why you don't want to marry."

"It's why I won't marry." He took a deep breath. "How many women would agree to never have children? Even if I find one who doesn't want kids, if I married her it would mean I'd made her my world. She'd be my family, and I don't want family. Not when there's a chance I'd lose it."

They stared at each other, the silence heavy between them.

He could see she wanted to argue. Her eyebrows were drawn together and her lips were pressed, and she looked at him with a mixture of sympathy and irritation.

Finally, she shrugged. "I can't tell you how to live. I think you're wrong. You're going to miss out on so much, but it's your life."

Chris nodded. His body felt heavy, weighted. It was out. Whatever happened moving forward, Sam was on notice.

"This doesn't change anything," he said. "I still want you and Maddie to stay with me. Even if I've just torpedoed any chance of something happening between us, I want you safe."

Sam looked out the window at her car. "I think you're overreacting. It's not so serious we have to move."

"Sam." He didn't say anything more. Just get his gaze steady on hers. He'd made up his mind. This was best.

She rubbed her forehead. "We'll come, but I hope you know what you're getting into."

The muscles in his back unclenched. He'd help her and Maddie move some stuff over after work. They'd be secure in his home. Protected.

As long as they were okay, he could deal with anything else.

Chapter Fifteen

SAM WIPED UP THE last of the marinara sauce on her plate with her wedge of bread. Chris's kitchen had been a dream to make dinner in, and cooking for him was the least she could do for him opening up his home to her and Maddie.

She looked at his plate as he wolfed down another bite of salad. He'd piled his plate mostly with greens with only a small section reserved for the pasta, the exact inverse of how Sam had filled her plate. It was a bit disconcerting being with a guy who ate healthier than her. It made sense in the job he was in, but he hadn't even had any garlic bread.

She shrugged. More of the good stuff for her.

Maddie stared down at a spot by her leg, and Sam pressed her lips together. They had a rule, no phones at the dinner table, but she obviously thought her sister was too dumb to notice.

"Hey." Sam jerked her chin at Maddie. "I cooked. You clean."

"Fine," she said in a voice that meant it was anything but. She stacked Sam's plate on top of her own then reached for Chris's. "You done?" She took his plate as he reached for the last bit of lettuce.

"I guess so." He tossed his fork on the plate and leaned back. "Thanks," he called after her retreating form. "And thank you." He turned to Sam. "Dinner was delicious."

"All you ate was a packaged salad mix. You barely had my pasta." Still, her body warmed, and it wasn't from the small glass of wine she was drinking. She liked feeding Chris, as stupid as that sounded. He was doing so much to try to take care of her. She wanted to reciprocate.

Chris's lips curled up devilishly. The warmth in her body settled somewhere lower. "Yes, but you opened that bag and mixed the ingredients like a pro," he said.

Sam laughed. It felt like forever since she'd been so happy and relaxed, and it was all due to being with Chris. She leaned back in her chair and swirled the little bit of wine left in her glass. "So why does a single guy have such a big house?" She looked around the combined living/dining room. The ceilings were high, giving the impression of even more space. To the left, a short hallway led to the master suite. The remaining three bedrooms were on the other side of the house, a smart layout if the parents wanted a little privacy from their kids.

Her hand stilled. Of course, that wouldn't be an issue for Chris.

Chris pushed his chair back at an angle so he faced her. "I was only planning on living here while I renovated the place. I flip houses as a side gig, though with the time it takes me to remodel a building, it has to be a really good deal in order for me to make any profit." He glanced at the wide brick fireplace in the living room. "I ended up liking this house so much, I decided to stay."

Sam could understand why. The house wasn't ostentatious, but it was roomy and comfortable and had every convenience a person could want. A kitchen a professional chef would envy, tons of closet space, and a hot tub on the back patio she couldn't wait to try out.

"You fixed this place up yourself?" She shook her head. Maybe it hadn't needed much work to begin with. She was having a hard time wrapping her mind around the snarky, irreverent Chris being dedicated enough for renovations. But the snarky, irreverent Chris wouldn't have taken her and Maddie into his house, either. Had she misread him all this time, or did he keep large parts of himself hidden?

He shifted. His leg pressed against hers under the table. Neither of them moved away. "My dad was a contractor. I spent a lot of summers working for him."

"My stepfather's a contractor, too." He'd never done anything to help fix up her mom's place, though. The fact that Chris had found the time for remodels outside his other duties was impressive. "You never thought of going into that business? Following in your father's footsteps?"

Chris ran his thumb along the rim of his water glass.

The motion was mesmerizing. Her skin tingled, as though feeling that phantom touch itself.

"I was a freshman in college when Paul died," he said. "I wanted to get away from everything familiar. Wanted my life to have more meaning. So I dropped out, enlisted in the Marines, and haven't looked back."

Maddie strode through the archway from the kitchen. "I'm going to my room," she said, sounding as comfortable as though she'd always lived here.

Sam raised her voice to follow her sister down the hall. "Make sure to finish your homework before—"

Her door slammed.

"—bed." She sighed. "I think she's trying to drive me crazy. Mad knows she'll get ownership of my *Dr. Who* DVD collector's edition if I do."

"*Dr. Who?*" Chris chuckled. "I wouldn't have taken you for a fan. I could never get into that show."

"Who played the doctor when you watched? Tennant? Capaldi?"

Chris raised his hands, palms up.

"Well, this has to be remedied." He would like *Dr. Who*. Some might prefer one iteration over another, but it had something for everyone. "Next time I'm home, I'll pick up a few seasons."

His jaw hardened. "Don't go back to your apartment unless I'm with you."

"Chris—"

"I'm serious. Whoever is harassing you knows where you live. I, or one of the other guys, will pick you up from work to make sure you're not being followed here. I'm going to make sure you're safe."

Her chest felt tight and bubbly, like an unopened bottle of champagne just waiting to burst. Chris was a protector. Someone fully in her corner when she'd become used to going it alone.

She stood then slid onto his lap, winding one hand behind his neck.

He stopped breathing, going completely still, and Sam smiled. "I still think you're overreacting, but thank you. I feel bad now for all the times I verbally demolished you in our fights. If I'd known you were such a sweetie, I would have given you a handicap."

"That's how you remember it?" Chris wrapped his arm around her waist.

"Uh huh." She nibbled on his jaw, his five o'clock shadow rough against her lips.

His arm tightened about her. "What I said, about not wanting a permanent relationship, I meant it."

Sam leaned back. She rested her palm over his heart, feeling the steady beat. "I know." Her throat went thick. She couldn't believe she'd wanted to try to seduce him into something more. Like his reasons, his emotions, weren't worthy of her respect.

"I can't do serious," he said, voice hoarse.

Her hand drifted across his hard chest. She nodded. This already felt serious. Her heart ached knowing whatever they could have wouldn't last, but she wanted him enough to take whatever time he would give her. "I know," she whispered. "But I've been reminded a lot recently that life truly is short. I'm not asking for forever. Hell, maybe we'll suck in bed together and our chemistry will fizzle. But I don't want to fight our attraction anymore. I want to live life to the fullest. I want you."

Chris cupped her cheek, angled her head. He brought his mouth to hers, the touch butterfly soft, before running his tongue along the seam of her lips.

She opened as a shiver danced down her spine.

Chris kissed her like he meant it. Like all his words about them being nothing serious were bullshit.

Maybe that was just what her foolish heart wanted to believe.

He raised his head, his midnight blue eyes glittering. He stood with her in his arms. "One thing I know," he said, striding for his bedroom. "The sex is not going to suck."

Chapter Sixteen

CHRIS LOOSED HIS HOLD on her legs, letting Sam slide down his body until she stood next to his bed. The thin T-shirt she wore did nothing to block the feel of her curves as they pressed against him. He cupped her cheek. Everything about Sam was so soft, when he was so hard.

So very, very hard.

Sam shifted, her belly brushing the front of his pants, and the erection trapped within. "I can't believe this is really happening," she said in a hushed voice.

Thank fuck this was finally happening. He needed Sam close, safe in his house, but having her in his home without touching her would have been torture. He brushed a strand of hair off her face. He let his fingertips continue down, across her jaw, along her neck.

She arched, giving him more room, and he lowered his head and replaced his fingers with his lips. Her scent, something sweet mixed with heated skin, was intoxicating. He breathed deeply as he scored her flesh with his teeth, dragging them gently down her throat.

Sam inhaled sharply and pressed her body closer. "You're wearing too many clothes." She fumbled with his shirt.

Chris grabbed the back collar and yanked it over his head in one motion.

"Wow." She pressed her palms to his chest then eased them down his abs, caressing every muscle and tendon.

"You've seen it before on the beach." But he couldn't deny he stood a little straighter. He kept his body fit for his work, but having Sam admire him was reason enough for his grueling workouts.

"Yeah, but looking and touching are two very different things." She bit her lower lip, her thumb brushing over his nipple. "Now I feel bad I don't eat more salad," she said pertly.

He'd seen her in a swimsuit, too, and knew there wasn't one inch of her he didn't desire. He slid his hand under her shirt, enjoying the feel of her silky skin against his palm. "You can eat whatever you want, but if you want to get more exercise, I'll let you do all the work the first time."

She raised one eyebrow. "This isn't what I... wait. The first time? How many rounds are you planning tonight?"

He dragged her shirt up and over her head. A pale purple bra covered her breasts, and his mouth watered. He pulled one cup down until her dark nipple popped over the fabric. "As many as your body can take." He bent and sucked the small berry into his mouth. He paid her other breast the same attention, loving how she gripped his hair, arched her back. "I'm trained for high physical intensity." He nibbled on the soft skin underneath. "As you're a civilian, I know I have to go easy on you."

She tugged his head up. Her eyes had a slightly glazed look to them, but that didn't keep them from narrowing in challenge. "I can take anything you give me."

His cock throbbed. With his hand above her heart, he pushed her onto the bed and crawled on top of her. "We'll see about that." She opened her mouth, no doubt to protest, call him a dirty name, but he covered that pretty mouth with his instead.

Their tongues tangled, sparred. They'd fought most of the time they'd known each other, so having it carry over into bed didn't surprise Chris. It did surprise him how much he liked it.

Too impatient with the clasp, Chris tugged her bra up and off like a shirt. Her breasts jiggled delightfully. Chris groaned, cupping one, and inched down the bed. He could spend hours on her breasts. Not too big, not too small, they were just right.

She tugged at his hair again. "Chris," she pleaded.

He ignored her, and continued further south. He brushed his lips along her ribs. He dipped his tongue into the hollow of her belly button.

She sucked in a gasp, and he made a note to explore that further. Later.

He popped open the button on her jeans, slid the zipper down, and dragged the denim from her legs.

He paused, drinking her in. God, she was gorgeous. Sam wore nothing but purple panties and a soft smile. She was here, in his bed, and nothing felt more right. He kept his gaze on her body, avoiding her eyes. It also felt very, very wrong.

He shouldn't be doing this, not with Sam. Not when he knew nothing more would come from it. She'd said she was okay with temporary, but he didn't know if she meant it.

He didn't know if he meant it, either.

But it was the way it had to be. The path he'd decided for his life long ago.

Ignoring the tightness in his chest, he pressed his face to the gusset of her panties, inhaling her musky scent. Fuck, she smelled good. He ripped the panties down her legs then settled in between her thighs. He swiped his tongue up her cleft and growled. She tasted even better.

She reached for his hair again. "Chris, I...."

Grabbing her wrists, he pinned them to her side. He made sure his shoulders blocked her legs from closing. "You'll lie there and take it, like a good girl." He set his mouth on her.

"Oh, God," she breathed, her thighs tense around him.

He smiled as he nosed her clit. Sam had given him enough tongue-lashings over the course of their relationship. It was time he repaid the favor.

He took long, leisurely swipes, from her opening to her clit and back down again.

Sam pulled at her wrists, but he didn't let her go. He needed to retain control, over her, over his emotions, over what was happening between them. This was just sex. But damned if he wasn't going to make it the best sex Sam had ever had.

He nibbled her folds before plunging his tongue into her channel. He thrust in and out, his hips rocking into the mattress, his dick eager to get in on the action. He worked her pussy until Sam started babbling, then sucked her clit into his mouth.

She arched off the bed and almost pulled from his grip. Her thighs squeezed his shoulders as tight as a python. "Oh, God, oh, God, oh, God," she wailed.

Her cries went straight to his groin. He couldn't wait any longer. Rearing up, he shucked the rest of his clothes off and reached for the box of condoms in his nightstand and tore one off. He had it rolled on before Sam had even caught her breath.

She reached for him. She cupped the back of his neck and drew him down, taking his mouth in a greedy kiss.

Chris returned it, wanting to devour her. It was rough, hot, desperate. When Sam raised her hips to him, lifting her knees to his hips, he couldn't deny himself any longer.

He notched his crown at her opening and pushed inside on one steady glide. Wet heat welcomed him, and nothing had ever felt so good.

Sam's lungs stalled. It seemed to take forever until Chris bottomed out. Her inner walls were deliciously stretched, the feeling of fullness almost too much.

"All right?" Chris's voice rumbled through her, making her skin tingle.

Or maybe it was the fact that Chris was inside her that was too much. Chris, the man she'd loathed and lusted after in equal measure. The man who'd wormed his way into her affections. In under a month, she'd become closer to him than anyone in her past.

Her throat felt too raw to speak so she nodded. Almost everything about this moment was perfect.

He pulled out slowly until only the tip of him remained inside her then plunged back home. He continued the same pace, an achingly unhurried retreat, followed by a forceful thrust.

Sweat beaded on her skin. She tried to increase the tempo, needing more, but he gave her enough of his weight to keep her pinned in place.

"Please," she moaned.

"You'll get there." Chris firmed his jaw. "But we're not hurrying this."

She tensed her inner muscles, clutching at his length as he eased back.

His eyes flared. "Sam," he said, a warning in his voice.

She scraped her teeth over her bottom lip. A bit of her old competitiveness sparked to life. She would make him lose control. She scratched her nails down his back and gripped his butt. The muscles flexed beneath her hands. It was the firmest ass she'd ever had the pleasure to hold.

Chris groaned. He lowered fully onto her, grinding his pelvis into her clit as he reached back first with one hand, then the other, and took her wrists. Breathing heavily, he pinned them by her head. "Not everything is on your schedule."

"Are you sure about that?" She locked her heels behind his back and clenched her channel again. She couldn't have a future with this man. Couldn't let this moment have the emotional depth her heart secretly craved. The least she could have was another fast and hard orgasm.

His eyes burned her. He laced his fingers with hers and squeezed. The connection between them felt so real. So deep. Her heart squeezed along with his grip. Sometimes life just wasn't fair.

Chris shifted his leg, pressing her thigh up higher. His next stroke hit a part in her she didn't think any other man had ever reached. Her eyes slid shut. And sometimes she thought too damn much.

He plunged into her with hard, fast strokes that stole her sense. Her muscles coiled, tighter and tighter. Pleasure hummed through her body. She bucked against him, climbing the peak higher and higher.

"Get there," Chris said through clenched teeth.

Her mind wanted to argue, to tell him that was out of her control if he kept hold of her hands. Her body told her to shut up and listen to the man.

He hammered into her, once, twice more, and she fell off the edge. Her body writhed as ecstasy exploded through her, from her eyelids to her toes. She curled and sank her teeth into his shoulder, needing to mark him as he had her.

His mark on her wasn't visible, but it was there nonetheless.

Chris pushed into her for several more seconds before he held himself deep. He threw his head back and made a sound that came deep from his chest.

He rocked slowly into her as his breathing evened. "Christ." He looked down at her, his gaze slightly wild. "That was...."

"Yes." She tightened her hold on his hands.

His Adam's apple bobbed. He looked away and sucked in a deep breath. When he looked back, his eyes were shuttered. "I told you it wouldn't suck," he said lightly. He pulled from her body and rolled away. Gripping the condom at the base of his cock, he retreated to the bathroom.

Sam slid under the covers and pulled the sheet to cover her breasts. Then she thought better of it.

Chris strode from the bathroom.

"Do you want me to go to my bedroom?" she asked. Sex was one thing. Sleeping in the same bed was another. Until Chris, she hadn't realized how much she'd taken for granted in past relationships. Of course, her boyfriends and her had slept in the same bed. That's what people who cared for each other did.

"Hell, no." He waggled his eyebrows. "I've got a couple more rounds in me tonight."

The ice in her soul warred with the instinctive heat that comment produced in her body. She smiled as he climbed into bed next to her, but it felt tight, distorted.

She lay back, her shoulder brushing his. They were so close, and she'd never felt so alone.

She sent a plea up to the universe. She wanted Chris to realize that life wasn't something to be guarded against. That experiencing heartache was worth the risk for a chance at happiness.

She turned on her side, facing away from him, and blinked back tears. She couldn't stand thinking that Chris might die an old man only having lived half a life. Even if it wasn't with her, she wanted him to know love.

When it came to her and Chris, however, she feared that it was already too late.

Chapter Seventeen

"WHY DO I HAVE to do it if she isn't?" Maddie whined, pointing at her sister lying in the sand twenty feet away.

"Because you were drinking while under age, because you got in a car with a drunk driver behind the wheel, because you were arrested by the police." Chris crossed his arms over his chest, trying like hell to stay focused on Maddie. Sam had run maybe a mile with the guys and her sister before bogeying out, but that had been plenty of time for sweat to make her skin glisten. For her thin T-shirt to cling to her curves.

The woman in question stretched her arms above her head, her back arching as she yawned.

Chris took a deep, satisfied breath. If Sam was moving a little slower than usual this morning, he prided himself that he was the one responsible. He had kept her very busy the night before. Busy, and blissed out.

He rubbed the back of his neck. Physically, he and Sam made an explosive pair. But he'd noticed the shadows in her eyes when he'd pulled back emotionally.

So he'd fucked her harder.

"You have to admit those are solid points," Travis said. He and the rest of the guys had decided to join Chris and

Maddie's boot camp for their morning PT. "You really screwed up, kid."

Maddie scowled. "It's not like I'm the only person who's ever made a mistake."

"Yeah, but you made three in quick succession," Tony pointed out. "And your only punishment is getting in better physical shape. I think Chris is going easy on you. Right, Chris? Chris?"

"Huh?" Chris dragged his gaze from Sam's body. The little minx was idly dragging her toes up and down her calf, something that Chris couldn't imagine finding sexy until Sam did it. "Oh, right, yeah. Let's get back to it. Fifty burpees, Maddie."

"If you position yourself in front of him, you can kick sand back in his face," Travis said, grinning.

Maddie groaned and flopped to the ground in the worst burpee form Chris had ever seen. He decided to keep that thought to himself, however. She was doing as she was told, and for now, that was enough.

"I don't want to stay at your house anymore," Maddie puffed out. "At least at Sam's I have the option of sleeping through my alarm."

Ryan paused in the push-up position to arch an eyebrow at Chris. "They're staying with you?"

"Yep." Chris started his own set of burpees. They really were a miserable exercise. "I couldn't let Maddie sleep through her boot camp."

Maddie hopped to her feet then staggered. "Very funny. It's because someone's been harassing Sam," she told Ryan. "They're afraid it will escalate." She frowned at the sand before collapsing back down and doing something that looked more like upward dog than a push-up.

Jake went to Chris's side. In a low voice, he said, "Caroline told me about Sam's car. How bad do you think it's getting?"

A tampered-with car. Some destruction with a key. Someone on the fire escape outside her home. It wasn't anything the cops would spend much time investigating. And yet....

"I know you're the one with a sixth sense, but I have a bad feeling about it." Chris turned his back to Maddie, wanting to keep her from hearing. With the way she was gasping and moaning with each burpee, it shouldn't be hard.

He looked at Sam, the skin on his chest pulling tight. She was laughing as she read something on her phone. She should be this carefree all the time. He hated that she had to worry about someone hurting her. Felt murderous at the thought of someone actually hurting her.

"I just...." He cleared his throat. "I need to keep her close. Safe."

Jake's eerie green eyes locked on him. He nodded. "Understood. Whatever I can do to help, name it."

"Are you sure someone is going after Sam?" a soft voice asked.

Chris whipped around. Maddie had her butt planted in the sand, her arms wrapped around her knees. She didn't take her eyes off the ocean.

Ryan scooted to sit next to her. "Hey, you don't have to worry. Chris and the rest of us will make sure your sister is safe."

Chris crouched by her side. "That's right. But you can help. Don't tell anyone where you guys are staying, not even your friends. If one of us isn't picking you up from school, take a different route when you walk back to my place each day. Be aware of your surroundings at all times."

"Jesus, Chris." Tony handed Maddie a bottle of water he'd pulled from the cooler. "Way to scare her." He placed his hand on her shoulder. "You and Sam will be fine."

Jake shrugged. "That sounded like solid life advice to me."

"Thank you." Chris glared at Tony. He loved his friend, but the man would coddle a woman right into the grave.

"But are you sure it's *Sam* this guy's after?" Maddie asked again. "Watching us from the fire escape...." A small tremor shook her body.

Blood pounded in Chris's ears. When he found this asshole, he was going to make him hurt. The same anger was mirrored in his friends' eyes. Their job was to safeguard the innocent. And when it was someone they knew and cared for who was threatened, who was scared, their instinct to protect went into overdrive.

Chris let his ass hit the sand. He wrapped his arm around Maddie's shoulders and squeezed her to him. "You don't have to worry." Great, now he was turning into Tony, but he couldn't stand seeing Maddie scared. "Sam is safe. *You* are safe. It's going to be okay."

Ryan nudged her knee. "Yeah, you've got five very protective older brothers now. No one's gonna hurt you."

Chris's muscles locked. His lungs stuttered to a stop. *Brother*. He thought of his squad members as brothers, but that was different than how it had been with Paul. They were all adults, more than capable of taking care of themselves. But Maddie....

She leaned against him, just the slightest bit, as though wanting his comfort but wary of taking it.

He tried to fight it, but just like her sister, Maddie had snuck under his defenses. He did feel like her brother.

And maybe that wasn't as bad as he'd thought.

Maybe it didn't have to be all or nothing. Maybe he could let them in. Just a little.

Jake pulled off his shirt. "Let's get our swim in. I assume Maddie is done for the day?"

Chris nodded. Torturing the girl on land was one thing; on the water it would be dangerous. "Boot camp is done for the day. And you still have time for a shower before school."

She groaned, but it was a normal, teenager sort of protest. Everyone hated going to school. The darkness in her eyes had disappeared.

"We heading out?" Sam strolled over, brushing sand off the seat of her shorts. She gave the rest of the guys an appreciative look as they took off their shirts, something Chris didn't care for. She made up for it when he pulled his off. Her eyelids lowered. She sucked her bottom lip into her mouth and looked like she wanted nothing more than to drag him back into bed.

Needing to hold her again, Chris stepped forward and swept her into his arms. "Maddie's called dibs on the shower, so I thought I'd help you get cleaned up." He ran for the water, her shrieks filling him with glee.

"Don't you dare drop me." Sam gripped his neck. She tried to sound stern but failed miserably. "If even one bit of me meets the ocean, I will make you pay, Corporal Gunn."

"What if I like how you make me pay?" he whispered in her ear.

Jake shook his head as he stomped past them before diving into the surf. The rest of the squad followed.

"That is a symptom of a very disturbed mind." Sam nipped his jaw.

He'd been accused of worse.

Chapter Eighteen

SAM'S STOMACH GROWLED. LOUDLY. Flushing, she looked around her office, but no one was near enough to hear. She reached for her desk drawer before remembering she hadn't packed a lunch that day.

She dropped her chin into her palm. Her routine was all messed up now that she was staying at Chris's. Not that she was complaining. Evening, morning, and middle of the night sex was well worth a forgotten PB&J or two, but all the extra workouts Chris had been putting her through made her extra hungry. And then he'd had the audacity to ask if she wanted to join them for PT again that morning.

The answer to that was a hell no and never again.

Her stomach made its displeasure known once more, and Sam stood, grabbing her purse. She dropped a report off to the mayor then hurried outside.

"You getting lunch?" Casey sat on a bench by the entrance. He slid his vape away and rose to his feet as she exited the building.

"Yep, I'm starving."

"Me, too," he said. "Mind if I come along?"

She smiled tightly. She didn't have a good reason to say no, and besides, it was just lunch. Casey was a nice guy, and they'd had lunch before. "Sure." She turned for the sidewalk, slowing until he fell into step next to her. "I was thinking the deli or Thai. Which do you prefer?"

"The Thai place has a nice outdoor patio."

Decision made, they strolled to the restaurant. It was a beautiful day, and sitting outside in the warm sun made the knots in Sam's shoulders relax. The only thing that would have made it more perfect was if she had been dining with Chris instead of a coworker.

"There's another concert in the park. Reggae this time." Casey took a sip of his ice tea. "Want to go?"

A very persistent coworker.

Sam slid her hand along her napkin. "Casey, I'm seeing someone."

His jaw set. "That guy in the parking lot?"

"Yes. Chris." She scraped her teeth over her bottom lip. Was she using Chris as an easy out to decline Casey's invitation? Yes, yes she was. Technically, she and Chris weren't dating. They were friends, kind of, he was protecting her, and they were fucking. He'd made the limits of their non-relationship very clear and she wanted to respect them.

But it felt like they were dating. She couldn't imagine seeing anyone else, not when her feelings were so entwined with Chris. When he smiled at her, her heart fluttered like a kaleidoscope of butterflies all taking flight at once. When he grew serious, worrying over her safety, she wanted nothing more than to ease his cares. And when his eyes darkened to midnight when he gave her *that* look.... Well, that's when she knew she'd give him everything.

The problem was he didn't want her everything.

She pushed aside her chicken curry, nausea coiling through her belly.

Casey nodded, and focused on his meal. The tight grip on his fork and spoon told her all she needed to know about his mood. She hated disappointing him. Hated even more that she knew it would never happen between them. She should be keeping her options open. And Casey would be a smart choice for her to explore.

She wanted all the things Chris didn't. Family. Connection. A love so big it could break you if lost.

They didn't have a future. If she wasn't such a dumbass, she'd end things with him now, give herself some time to heal, and move on.

But she was a dumbass when it came to Chris. Had been from the moment they'd met and had hidden it as best she could with snark and biting remarks. The adult version of pulling the hair of the boy you like.

"It's serious?" Casey asked.

Sam blew out a breath, slumping in her chair. "It is for me," she said sadly.

He nodded, and they finished their meals. There wasn't much left to say. They paid and started the walk back to work.

"I do hope you're happy." Casey shoved his hands in his pockets. "This guy better treat you right."

Sam smiled. Casey really was a good guy. She hoped after all this they could still be—

Light blinded her. She threw up a hand to block the glare as tires screeched on pavement. She blinked, and the hood of a car filled her vision as it hopped the sidewalk and barreled toward them.

Someone screamed. Casey dragged his gaze from his feet, his mouth slowly widening into a shocked O.

Sam pressed her hands to his side and pushed him into the entrance nook of the business they were passing. Her momentum took her the other way. She leapt for the car parked next to her, hoping to squeeze as much of her body between it and the curb as she possibly could.

A roar filled the air. A crack pierced her eardrums. Something dark blue hurtled toward her as she fell.

Her last thought before the object struck her was that it was the same color as Chris's eyes.

Chapter Nineteen

CHRIS GATHERED UP HIS parachute and headed for the hangar. He'd been the last one out of the plane, and now the last one to join the after-training review. Since they'd trained on HALO jumps many times before, however, there wasn't much to say.

"It was gusty up there." Jake had one hip cocked on the equipment table. "You need to adjust your jump time according to wind speed, Viper."

Tony nodded, his lips pressed flat. He'd been the only man to land out of the target zone, though it hadn't been by much. He was a Squid. It shouldn't surprise anyone he was more comfortable in the water than in the air.

"Any other issues we need to address?" Jake turned his head to Chris as he plopped his parachute and harness on the table.

"It was all good for me," Chris said. Falling out of a plane was as easy as breathing to Chris, especially when they jumped in broad daylight.

"Then lets head back to base." Jake stood, stretched. "I hope to get out of there early tonight. Caroline and I have plans."

Ryan made a whipping sound. "Our ranks are falling," he said to Tony and Travis. "First Jake and now Chris is living with someone."

"I'm not living with anyone." In point of fact, Sam was living with him. And as much as he wanted it to, her being in his house didn't suck. In fact, waking up with her in his bed was a treat he was becoming used to. When she left, it would hit him as hard as a strict calorie diet.

Which was fine. He was disciplined. He could take it.

The men ignored him.

"You've jinxed yourself now." Travis elbowed Ryan. "You're next."

Ryan's face blanked. "That's not going to happen."

Chris snorted. If anyone was more allergic to commitment than he was, it was Ryan.

His phone rang, and he couldn't stop the smile as he saw Sam's name.

"She's even calling to check up on him now." Ryan shook his head.

Chris picked up his duffle and answered. "Hey, Sam. What's up?" he asked as he strode for the door.

"Uh, it's not Sam," a decidedly masculine voice answered.

Chris halted. "Who are you? Where's Sam?" His low growl brought his friends to his side, looking concerned.

"This is Casey, Sam's coworker. I got Sam's phone when they took her to the hospital."

His legs started moving again. He smashed the door open. "What happened? What hospital?" His legs ate up the distance to his truck. The rest of his squad was at his back.

"Jacksonville Memorial." Casey cleared his throat. "There was an accident. A car.... God, she hasn't woken up yet."

Chris's breaths rasped in his lungs. Pain lanced his chest. "I'll be there in twenty." He cut off the call. He turned wild eyes on his friends. "I need—"

"Go," Jake said. "We heard enough."

Chris threw his bag in the truck and jumped behind the wheel. "Can someone get Maddie?"

Jake pulled out his phone. "Caroline and I will. She's an approved person to pick her up from school."

Nodding, Chris started the engine and peeled out of the parking lot. He couldn't get a full breath. It felt like a giant hand had wrapped around his lungs and squeezed.

Sam would be okay. This wouldn't be a repeat of—

He slammed his palm on the steering wheel. "God damn it," he roared. This wouldn't happen to him again. Sam would be fine. She'd laugh at how worried he'd been. Tell him he was overreacting. That she just had a few scratches.

She hadn't woken up yet.

His head grew light as his breathing increased. He forced himself to slowly fill his lungs, slowly empty them. He was a god-damned Raider. He didn't hyperventilate.

Chris didn't know if the parking spot he found near the entrance to the ER was painted red, yellow, or green. He didn't care. The automatic doors barely slid open in time to admit him as he raced inside.

His gaze lasered in on the man he recognized from the front of city hall. Casey was talking to a cop in uniform, his hair a mess as he ran his hand through it. His eyes held pity when he caught sight of Chris storming up.

"How is she?"

Casey shrugged. "I haven't heard anything yet."

The cop looked him up and down. "And you are?"

"Corporal Chris Gunn."

"Her boyfriend," Casey added.

Boyfriend. What a useless term. It held zero depth, did nothing to convey the way he felt about Sam. He'd wanted to avoid becoming Sam's boyfriend, avoid the entanglements, and somehow he had leap-frogged right over it into whatever the hell kind of relationship he and Sam now had. It was nothing so insipid as boyfriend and girlfriend.

"There was a hit-and-run." The cop was brisk and to the point. "A car jumped the curb. It hit a mailbox which struck Ms. Winters."

"I didn't see it happening until it was too late." Casey closed his eyes. "She pushed me out of the way. The sound when the mailbox hit her...."

Chris clenched his hands. He wouldn't let himself think about that now. "What kind of car? Did you see who was driving?"

Casey remained silent.

The cop flipped her notepad shut. "Mr. Greenberg was unable to identify either, except to say the car might have been gray." She cocked her head. "You don't think this was a random accident?"

Chris shook his head. "You'll find police reports Sam has made for previous incidents of harassment. They were minor compared to this, but no, I think this was targeted." And whoever had done this had just become Chris's target. He wouldn't rest until he found the scumbag and made him pay.

The officer took down Chris's contact information, wished him well, and left.

Casey sank down into a chair.

Chris paced.

She hasn't woken up yet.

He received texts from his friends, but as he had no news to update them with, didn't respond.

Finally, a nurse emerged from the back and approached Casey. "Are you Chris?"

Chris stepped forward. "I am. Is she okay?"

"She'll be fine. She needs rest, and we want to keep her overnight for observation. She's asking for you."

The nurse led him back to the exam rooms. He had to keep himself from tripping over her heels. She moved too slowly, and he had zero patience left.

Sam gave him a wobbly smile when the nurse led him to her room.

His heart stalled before breaking into a gallop. The right side of her face was swollen and bruised. She had a sling on her right arm. But she was alive. Alive, awake, and absolutely precious.

He dragged a chair to her side and sat before his legs gave out. Gently, he took her free hand. "How are you feeling?"

"Like I've just been steamrolled." She rested her head back on the bed, as though it were too tiring to hold it up. Her eyes were liquid as she gazed at him. "But I'll be fine. They still need to take me to X-ray for my shoulder, but I don't think anything is broken."

He scooted closer. The only thing keeping him from crawling onto that narrow bed with her was the knowledge he'd probably hurt her if he did. "You're too hard-headed for anything above the neck to be broken, that's for sure."

Her eyes fluttered closed. "Everyone knows you're the stubborn one," she murmured. Her chest rose and fell in a steady pattern.

All the tension in Chris's body released. He couldn't take his eyes off of that small proof of life. She breathed. She lived. He'd never understood what a gift life was until that moment.

"Any chance that was a drunk driver?" she asked, her voice small.

"I don't think so." He kissed the back of her hand.

A tear escaped from the corner of her eye and slid down her cheek.

Using his thumb, he brushed it away. If he had the power to brush away all her problems, he would. "I don't want you to worry. You just need to rest and get better."

She gave him a small nod, but like most things, he knew it was easier said than done. He'd told himself enough times that he'd be able to keep Sam at arms' length. Be able to fuck her, have fun, then move on.

He threaded his fingers through hers. All his plans for a safe, orderly, unemotional life had gone up in flames. And there was nothing he could say to himself to return to the person he'd been before Sam.

Chapter Twenty

SAM GUSTED OUT A breath, longing for the idyllic time when she'd been unconscious. She stared at the ceiling tile above her hospital bed. Was it loose? Could it fall on her head and take her away from this torture? She wasn't that lucky.

"I posted it all over my social medias," her mom continued. "If anyone saw who did this, I'll find out." Her chin wobbled. "My poor baby," she wailed.

Frank patted her shoulder and pressed a fountain soda cup into her mother's hand. She took a noisy sip of what Sam hoped was just pop, but suspected had something else mixed in.

"I'm okay, Mom." She rubbed her temple gently, the pounding on the inside of her head now matching the throbbing on the outside. It wasn't that she minded that her mom was upset. It felt good that her mom gave a damn for once. But did she have to be so loud about her caring?

"This has been very upsetting for your mother." Frank leaned forward in his chair. "For everyone. Maddie must be scared to death. We'll take her home with us tonight. Be there for her."

"Mad is staying with Caroline tonight. They already left for their movies and brownie sundae marathon." Sam sniffed.

She couldn't deny she was feeling the presence of that little green-eyed monster. She'd so much rather be curled up with Maddie and Caroline than stuck in the hospital with her mom and Frank. Especially since Caroline made the best brownies. They'd better save her some.

Frank's nostrils flared. "She should be with family," he said reproachfully.

"Caroline is family to us." Sam let her eyes close for a couple of seconds. Her body felt so heavy, as though the thin mattress could suck her down into it. Luckily, her shoulder wasn't broken, just sore as hell. Having a one hundred pound mail box slam into you would do that, she guessed.

"A girl belongs with her mother." Frank's voice rose a notch.

Sam ignored him. She wanted three things right now, and was in enough pain that she was getting surly about not having them. She wanted Chris. She wanted her mom and Frank to leave. And she wanted to rest.

Chris, at least, would be back soon. He'd promised, and Sam knew he was a man who kept those. He'd gone home to pack a bag. Her hospital room had a bench that pulled out into a small visitor's bed, and he was planning on using it tonight.

When her mom had swooped in, making enough noise about her 'poor baby' to have woken the dead, Sam had seen one of his friends hovering by the door, standing guard, until Chris returned. She hadn't seen which man it was, but she'd felt better knowing Chris hadn't left her alone, even for a half an hour.

Someone had tried to kill her. A small tremor ran up her body. She wasn't quite sure how to handle that. How could someone hate her that much?

A warm, soft weight was laid atop her abdomen.

She dragged her eyes open. Chris stood above her, tucking another blanket around her body. "You're back," she said softly.

"I'm back." The corners of his eyes crinkled.

"And who the hell are you?" Her mom narrowed her eyes. "I thought you were an orderly at first, tiptoeing in here and giving her another blanket."

Sam inhaled sharply. Her mom was getting belligerent. Her cup definitely had something other than soda in it. She must also be going blind if she thought Chris, with his stretchy T-shirt and ripped muscles, was an orderly. Or maybe orderlies here worked out more than Sam thought. What was an orderly anyway? A nurse? A candy striper?

And now she was getting loopy.

"I'm Chris Gunn, a friend of your daughter's." His finger brushed along her arm, the soothing sensation almost enough to make up for the use of the word *friend*. "She needs her rest, but don't worry, I'll stay with her."

"You'll stay with her?" her mother's voice rose.

"Yes, Mom. I want Chris here." Sam tried to make her voice forceful, but she was exhausted. "I'll call you tomorrow, okay?"

Her mom puffed up, like a roosting hen about to let an intruder have it.

Frank waved her down. "Don't get worked up, Denise. Let the kids be." He turned and planted his hands on his hips. "But we're not leaving without Maddie. She needs to come home."

"Maddie needs parents she can trust." Chris's tone was civil but as firm as his abs. "If Denise can clean her act up, maybe Maddie will go home, but right now it's not a good place for her."

"You little prick," her mom said as Frank blustered. "How dare you! You have no right to talk to us like that."

"And no right to keep Maddie from her mother," Frank said tightly.

Sam's jaw dropped. There was being direct, and then there was Chris's version of being direct. It was like a matchstick compared to a nuclear weapon.

Chris crossed his arms over his wide chest. "When it comes to children, I don't care about rights. I care about doing what's best, and I'm making it my responsibility. It's time for you to leave."

Sam blinked up at him, her heart doing a triple-beat. When Chris wanted to turn it on, he turned it *on*. And the fact he was going all protective over her little sister, well, that did things to her. It was too bad she was too sore and tired to show him how amazing she thought he was.

The door swung open, and Travis poked his head inside. "Everything okay in here?" His usually smiling mouth was set in a hard line.

"Everything's fine," Chris said. "Sam's mom and stepfather were just leaving."

Frank opened his mouth to protest again, but Chris cut him off. "Sam needs quiet. She's going to get it." There was a definite threat hanging in those words, and Frank and her mom were smart enough to heed it.

"We'll talk tomorrow," her mom said, hefting her purse on her shoulder and holding tight to her cup.

Frank said nothing, just stomped after his wife.

Travis stepped to the side and held the door for them. After they'd left, he turned. "You good for the night?"

"Yeah." Chris pulled one of the guest chairs around the bed and plopped it next to her so he was facing the door. "We're good. Thanks, man."

"Anytime." Travis's body relaxed back into easy-going. One side of his mouth hitched upward. "Feel better, Sam." And then he was gone.

Leaving her alone with Chris.

She rubbed the edge of her blanket between two fingers. "Thank you for standing up for Maddie." The back of her throat burned. "It was more than I've ever done." Why hadn't she ever stood up to her mom like that? Told her to get her act together for Maddie's sake? She'd always thought of herself as a strong, take-charge kind of woman, but she'd been fooling herself. She'd wanted to avoid conflict more than do what was necessary to protect her sister.

"Bull." Chris rested his forearms on the bed next to her side. "You're providing a good, stable home for your sister."

She bit out a harsh chuckle. "Stable? She's been arrested, uprooted from her own bed because of some stalker, and is now visiting her sister in the hospital. Maybe she would be better off at home."

"None of that was your fault." He trailed his fingertips down her arm until he could lace his fingers with hers. He squeezed her hand.

The moment felt raw. Intimate. And Sam had to remind herself that this was just Chris being Chris. A champion. A caretaker. It didn't mean he'd given up his foolish ideas and wanted to settle down and make beautiful babies with her.

She turned her head away.

"Do you remember anything more about the car?" he asked.

"No." She sighed. "It's all just a blur."

He squeezed her hand again. "That's okay. We'll get him. You get some rest now."

That sounded like the best advice she'd heard all day. She was safe with Chris, her mom and stepdad were gone, and, finally, she could sleep.

She'd gotten her three wishes.

But she didn't feel fulfilled. She still yearned. She had one wish left, and it was a big one.

And according to Chris, it was never coming true.

Chapter
Twenty-One

CHRIS PADDED ON BARE feet toward the kitchen. Jake and Ryan had turned his spare bedroom into a makeshift command center and after hours of poring over data and leads, they all needed some fuel.

He passed the living room. Sam and Maddie sat on the sofa, their backs to him as they watched a movie. Sam had taken the sling off when she'd gotten home from the hospital, but she rested her arm on a pillow stacked on the armrest.

"I won't go back home," Maddie said in a low voice to Sam. "I know Mom and Frank have been nagging you—"

"Let me worry about them." Sam's shoulders were tight, and Chris wanted nothing more than to massage her tension away. Everything that Sam had been through was building up in her, and he worried. Sam was strong, but everyone had a breaking point.

Maddie rested her head on Sam's shoulder. "If they try and make me go back, I'll run away."

Chris muffled a groan and turned to the kitchen, knowing he'd intruded on their privacy too long. That was a threat that Sam definitely didn't need. But he couldn't say he blamed Maddie. Living with parents who always put their needs above their child's could be soul-sucking.

He made a large pile of sandwiches, grabbed some bottles of water, and juggled everything back to the guys.

Jake was just ending a call. "It's confirmed. The car was stolen. The police found it abandoned off Cole Road. They'll take it in for a full sweep, but there were no prints on any of the obvious places." Jake had developed contacts in the local force when Caroline had been in trouble. Chris had hoped they'd never have to use them again.

"From traffic cameras, ATMs, and a squirrel cam, I've managed to trace the asshole's route from McAllister to where the attack happened on Sam to Seabreeze, which isn't too far from Cole." Ryan rubbed his jaw. "I'm assuming he was on his way to dump the car when the cam footage ended."

Chris shot him a look. "Squirrel cam?"

"Someone set up a squirrel obstacle course that has 24/7 webcam...." Ryan shook his head. "You know what, don't ask. Just know that if you ever need video of the corner of Oceanway and Park, you can get it."

"And the other video?" Jake arched an eyebrow. "Traffic cameras and bank ATMs? *Private* bank ATMs?"

"Yeah... don't ask about that, either." Ryan's fingers flew over his keyboard. He brought an image up on one of the three monitors he'd set up for his computer. "This still is the best look we have of the driver. And to say it's not great is an understatement. I doubt even this guy's mother would recognize him."

Chris planted his palm on the desk and leaned close to the screen. The image was grainy, but clearly showed a man holding tight to the steering wheel with both hands. "He's wearing a fucking surgical mask."

"And with the hoodie and sunglasses...." Ryan blew out a breath. "It's a dead end."

Chris smashed his fist onto the desk. "Son of a bitch." They had nothing. He had to tell Sam that his highly-skilled special forces team had jack shit, and she was still in danger.

"I'll send you the address the car was stolen from." Jake sent Ryan a text. "Maybe you can get something from that area."

"Residential?" Ryan asked.

Jake nodded.

Ryan grimaced. "There might be some home security video, but those don't typically record unless the motion sensor is tripped. Maybe we'll get lucky."

"I can't rely on luck," Chris bit out. "This is Sam's safety we're talking about. I need answers. Now." He was being an asshole; he knew it. His friends were doing everything they could to help. Tony was outside in his car keeping watch. Travis would take guard duty later. And Ryan was probably breaking fifteen laws getting video. But logic was not only out the window when he thought about Sam's near-miss, it was off the fucking planet.

He inhaled her sultry scent a moment before she wrapped her hand around his arm. "Chris." Sam's voice was equal parts chiding and sympathy.

Chris closed his eyes, trying to rein it in. He didn't lose his head over a woman. Ever. But Sam was a battle he was losing. He didn't even know if he wanted to engage in another action or surrender.

"Are you guys about done?" It was less a question Sam asked than a demand.

"Yes, ma'am." Jake grabbed a sandwich and saluted them with it. "See you tomorrow."

Ryan took the whole plate of sandwiches. "Have a good night." He smirked, and followed Jake out of the room.

When they were alone, Sam wrapped her arms around his waist. She nuzzled in against his back. "It's going to be all right."

He rested his hands above hers. "What are you doing?"

"Trying to comfort you?"

He huffed out a laugh. He turned in her arms until they were face to face. "That's my job."

She trailed her fingers over his jaw, lingering on his cleft. She bit her lip. "There's nothing to say we can't share in those responsibilities." Her eyes crinkled. "But there's one thing I believe I am uniquely qualified to do."

Sam's hair was up in a messy, little bun. He peeled the elastic from the top knot and shook her hair loose. He trailed the tips of his fingers over the lingering bruise on her face. "What's that?" he murmured.

Reaching back with her foot, she kicked the door closed. "Help relieve you of all this tension you're carrying." With a flirty little eyebrow waggle, she started to slide down his body.

He cupped her elbows, halting her progress. "You're sore."

"Not that sore." She bit his pec, her teeth sending shivers of delight across his skin even through his shirt.

"You don't have—"

"I know." She pulled free from his grip and continued down. "I want to."

Even through his shirt and jeans, her camisole and sleep pants, Chris could feel every inch of her body as it travelled across his. The friction made him ache. When her breasts brushed over his groin, he bit back an oath. When she pressed her cheek against his thigh, he fisted his hands.

This woman. She was everything. Which meant she could make him lose everything. The risk had never been worth it before.

She focused on his zipper as she dragged it down, her eyes glowing like her favorite prize lay hidden behind. When her soft, warm hand wrapped around his dick, a haze wrapped around his mind. His hips arched toward her, and she lowered her head, brushing her lips across his balls.

Chris groaned.

This woman. She was *everything*. And she could be his, if he could only let himself yield.

Sam rubbed her cheek along his length, inhaling his musky scent. She needed this. Needed time where it was just her and Chris, giving and taking pleasure. Time where she didn't have to think about how close she'd come to dying, or how her shoulder still throbbed with pain. Time where she didn't have to worry about Maddie, and how unhappy her sister had become.

She gently sucked one sac into her mouth, smiling as Chris cursed. This man was ripped with muscle, equipped with discipline and determination, and at the moment, she had the power to bring him to his knees.

She licked up his cock and suckled at the crown.

Chris dug his fingers into her scalp, and tugged. "Give me your eyes," he demanded, voice gruff.

She met his gaze as she took him deep. His sapphire eyes shimmered. He cupped her cheek, opening his mouth to speak. Whatever words he had turned into a groan as she flicked her tongue against his skin, sucking hard.

She gripped the base of his cock with one hand as she went down on him. In the past, giving head had only been about pleasing her partner. But with Chris's gaze locked with hers, the sound of his stuttering breath the only thing filling her ears, this felt like more. There was a connection. She'd felt it in the hospital when he'd held her hand like a drowning man did a life saver. She felt it now. She hadn't gone into this relationship intending to change Chris's mind about getting serious, but she couldn't help but hope that his mind had been changed nonetheless.

Chris nudged his hips forward, and she took him deeper. She wanted his surrender so badly, a mewl of distress escaped her mouth when he pulled out of her. He pulled her to her feet and crushed his mouth to hers. The kiss was greedy, consuming, and ended much too soon.

Chris yanked her sleep pants down, stopping to press his lips against the bruise on her hip, the one on her thigh. "Turn around."

It was an order, one she was happy to obey. She turned and rested her left forearm above her head on the wall.

Chris tugged her hips until her back arched and her ass lifted. He ran his hand down her spine then lower. His fingers glided between the seam of her cheeks. At her opening, he paused. With one blunt fingertip, he pressed inside, the smallest amount. He made shallow thrusts, lighting up all the nerve endings at her entrance but giving her no relief.

She tried to push back, but he stayed her with a hand at her hip. "Chris," she whispered, his name trailing off into a hiss. Her folds grew slick and something deep inside of her clenched. "Now," she begged.

He didn't leave her waiting. The broad head of his cock replaced his finger, and he pressed inside in one smooth stroke.

She almost came right there, the relief of being filled so great.

He held himself inside her. "Fuck. Condom. Feel so good."

Her lips curved. At least she wasn't the only one reduced to caveman language skills. "Don't care. On pill."

He groaned as he pulled from her. It took him only a moment to get his wallet from his sagging jeans and retrieve a condom.

She didn't want to analyze what that meant, his need for the barrier. There was nothing wrong with being safe, after all. And when he plunged back inside her, she stopped thinking altogether.

Sam bit her lip as Chris hammered into her. Maddie was only down the hall. Sam had to keep quiet. But damn Chris made it hard.

He braced his left arm above hers and slid his right hand around her hip to rest between her navel and her mound. His thumb swept underneath the hem of her camisole. He nosed her hair aside and licked the shell of her ear.

A shudder rippled through her body. It had never been this good before with anyone. It had to be more than just hormones and attraction between them.

He nibbled on her earlobe as he undulated behind her. Her core tightened. Her breath came in pants. She pressed her palm to Chris's hand and guided it lower.

He butterflied a touch over her clit as he snapped his hips, establishing a bruising pace. He grunted softly in her ear, heat rolling off his body. "Sam," he breathed, the word sounding like a prayer.

She shattered. Her sheath clamped down hard, causing Chris's stroke to falter. He powered through, extending her waves of pleasure until she went limp.

Chris buried his face in the curve of her shoulder, letting her skin muffle his shout as he came. He molded his body around her back. She could feel the thump of his heart, the rise and fall of his chest as he dragged in air.

She leaned her head against his. It was a moment of perfect bliss. One that was all feeling and no thought. Which was the only reason she had to explain her next words. "I love you, Chris."

He stopped breathing. Stopped moving entirely. And as the silence grew, all her hopes and dreams curled into a tight ball and burrowed so deeply within herself as to virtually disappear.

Chris peeled himself off of her. She had been so warm, and now the air against her back felt frigid.

She pulled her pants up, wishing she could hide her heart as easily as she could her bare ass. She forced her body to turn, her eyes to meet his. She even managed a lift to her chin. She would not be ashamed of how she felt.

And she wouldn't let Chris see he'd crushed her by not feeling the same way back.

He rid himself of the condom and righted his clothes. "Sam. I can't... I don't..." His gaze flicked away. "I'm sorry."

Fingernails dug into her heart. "No, I'm sorry." How could someone's words cause physical hurt? The ache in her shoulder was nothing in comparison to the pain in her chest. "You told me you only wanted casual."

"You're not casual." His nostrils flared. "I feel more for you than any other woman. I wish I could..." He shook his head. "I just can't."

She nodded, a pleasant numbness spreading from her abdomen out through the rest of her body. For the first time she truly understood Chris's position. Feeling nothing was so much better than the pain of losing the one thing she desired most.

She raised her eyebrows. Except she hadn't lost it. She'd never had it. "I should go."

"No." He narrowed his eyes. "Someone still tried to kill you. You're staying here until we catch the bastard."

She nodded again, her head feeling like it had been loosened from her neck. That made sense. No use getting dead just because it hurt to even look at Chris. "I'll stay, but in the guest room. I can't—" The backs of her eyes burned, and she sucked down a breath. "It appears I can't do casual. I was a fool to think I could."

He reached for her, but Sam side-stepped his hand. "Good night," she said before escaping.

She *had* been a fool. A fool for thinking there could be anything between her and Chris except foreplay fights and heat and irritation. Some sparks weren't meant to kindle into a fire.

She dropped onto the cold guest bed. And some fires sizzled out before they had ever truly begun.

Chapter
Twenty-Two

SAM SHIFTED ON THE hard seat at Chris's kitchen table. If she was going to work here for the next few days, as Chris and the rest of the guys insisted she should, she needed to find a better set-up.

"Where are you and Maddie?" Helen asked over the phone. "I haven't seen you in days."

Sam stared at the contract on the computer screen in front of her. She'd been looking at the same page for an hour. "We're staying with a friend right now." She was coming to hate the word *friend*. "We'll be back soon."

"And why aren't you calling me from the office phone." The older woman's voice was suspicious. She should have been a cop.

"I'm working from home today." Sam raked her hand through her hair. Thankfully, it was just her and Travis. She hadn't asked where Chris was going when he left. He hadn't told her. To say living with him until this was over was going to be awkward would be an understatement. She'd thought about asking Caroline if she could stay with her and Jake but didn't want to put her friend at risk.

"And you still got the job of calling me back." Helen chuckled. "You must be low man on the totem pole."

"No, they begged me to talk to you," Sam teased. "They'll owe me one."

"I'm a PITA," Helen agreed. "I know it, and I'm fine with it. I just don't want our town to slide into degeneracy. Which is why I want a police presence at Union Circle. I've seen drug deals going down there three times in the last month. It needs to stop."

"How do you know they were drug deals?" Sam's interest perked despite herself. She should talk to Helen every time she was in a miserable mood. Except, this wasn't just a bad mood. She had a feeling her heartache would last months. She'd actually thought Chris felt the same way about her. She'd relied on the way he looked at her, touched her, instead of the words coming out of his mouth.

She was such an idiot.

Helen sniffed. "Furtive looks. Small packages and money exchanging hands. It doesn't take Sherlock Holmes to figure it out."

"Okay." Sam opened up her email. "I'll send a message to the local PD. See if I can't light a fire under them to check it out."

"Thanks, Sam. I always know I can count on you."

Sam swallowed. At least someone appreciated her.

"Dinner at my place this Friday?" Helen asked.

"I'll let you know." She'd probably still be under house arrest. "Talk to you later," she said and disconnected.

Rising, she slowly stretched out her muscles. Too many parts of her were still tender from her faceoff with a mailbox, and the hard chair wasn't helping. She arched her back, feeling a soft pop, then bent at the waist, easing the strain on her lower back.

"Whoa." Travis's feet stopped in her field of vision between her legs.

Sam straightened, too depressed to care that she'd just given the man a primo view of her ass. She was wearing leggings and a tank top, wanting comfort. No dress code was a definite perk of working from home.

"Hey, what's up?" she asked.

"Tony's picking up some coffee on his way here." Travis ran a hand through his nutmeg hair. He kept his gaze studiously on her face. "Want anything?"

"No, thanks. I'm good." Sam tilted her head. "Can I ask you something?"

"Sure."

"Why aren't you seeing anyone?" She'd seen Jake's devotion to her friend and thought that would be the norm for his group of friends. But the rest were all single. Maybe Chris was the norm. Maybe there was nothing she could have done to tempt him into changing his mind. "You're good-looking, have a secure job. I'd think the women would be lining up."

"Still sowing those oats, I guess." He shifted on his feet and looked away. "Though I wouldn't mind what Jake has. What you and Chris are developing."

Spots appeared in Sam's vision, and she blinked. "We aren't developing anything. Chris and I...." She bit back the words 'just friends.' Frankly, they weren't even that. "We aren't any-thing."

Travis raised his eyebrows. "Then he's an idiot."

Her phone rang, and she reached for it. Why couldn't she have wanted Travis? Life would have been so much easier. "This is Sam Winters speaking." Her hand fluttered to the base of her neck as she listened. She swallowed. "Yes. All right. I'll let you know."

Travis straightened. "What's wrong?"

"That was Maddie's school." She looked at her phone, like the answers would appear on the screen. "They said she hasn't been to class since recess." Their conversation from the night before ran through her head. Would Maddie have run away? It didn't make sense. Sam had assured her she could live with Sam as long as she wanted.

Her muscles quivered. Was Maddie into ditching school, too? Now, when she knew there was some psycho after Sam, her sister would do something this foolish? She clenched her jaw. "I know some spots Maddie likes to hang out. Can we go check to see if she's there?"

Travis nodded. "I'll just let Chr— the other guys know what's up." He sent a text as they locked up and went to his car.

Sam gave him directions to the fast food restaurant near Maddie's school she thought was the most likely target. They were five minutes into the drive when her phone rang again. Her stepfather's name flashed on the screen.

"Frank," Sam said, "I don't suppose you've heard from—"

"Sam." Maddie's voice was a whisper choked out between sobs.

Sam jerked. "Maddie? What's wrong? Where are you?"

"At some construction site." Her voice broke. "I don't know where. Sam, you have to get me. You have to—"

Maddie shrieked. A scuffle sounded over the line. "Who the fuck is this?" a man asked.

Travis pulled the car over. He mouthed the word *speakerphone*.

Sam nodded and did as he asked. "Frank? Is that you?" she asked.

"Ah, if it isn't the interfering bitch." Something was wrong with Frank's voice. It was deeper than usual. Meaner. And the words were spit out bullet-fast.

"Why is Maddie with you?" Sam's heart thumped. She should be happy Maddie was with family. But something was wrong. "Why isn't she in school?"

"Maddie is where she belongs. With me." He crooned something softly away from the phone. Her sister's 'fuck off' came through loud and clear, however.

"This is your fault." Frank's accusing voice came back on the line. "You took her away from me. My sweet, little lady belongs with me."

Nausea coiled in her gut. Her brain refused to focus. Refused to let itself go there. All she knew was that Maddie was in trouble, and needed her. "Where the fuck are you?"

Travis placed his hand on her shoulder, gave her a warning squeeze.

"Why couldn't you just die?" Frank whined. "If you were dead, she'd have to come back to me."

Travis started texting furiously.

Sam tried to even her voice, but it was shaking as badly as her hands. "Frank, I need to see Maddie. Tell me where you are, and I'll come join you. We can talk this out."

"You need to stop coming between us." Frank panted into the phone. "Your mother didn't care about Maddie's and my special relationship, but you had to get in the way. I've waited long enough." The call ended.

"Frank? Frank?!" She dialed Frank back. It went straight to voicemail. Sam couldn't breathe. She gulped breaths, but no air seemed to flow into her lungs. She clutched Travis's arm. "Maddie... I need Maddie... We have to find her."

Travis shifted so he was facing her. "Easy there. Slow, deep breaths, okay? Ryan is running a trace on your stepfather's cell right now. We'll get her." He looked down at his phone, then pressed a button. "Chris wants to talk to you." He handed her his mobile, and she grabbed it like a lifeline.

"Chris?" Her voice rose.

"It's okay, baby." His deep tone rolled over her like honey, easing into all her broken parts and taking her heart rate from a sprint to a lope. "He didn't have time to take her far. She's close, and we'll find her."

"She said she was at a construction site."

Chris spoke to someone on his side before coming back on the line. "Okay, that helps. Who can we call in the city for a list of current builds?"

"I thought you were tracing his cell phone?"

Chris hesitated. "He might have taken out his SIM card. I want to have multiple ways to find her. Current build sites?" he reminded her.

Sam stared out the windshield. This was something she should know. Something she could help with. Her mind drew a blank. "Uh..."

"Someone with the permit department maybe?" Chris asked.

"Mindy. Mindy Grosse." Something nagged at her. It was mid-morning on a workday, and she hadn't heard a sound of construction when Maddie had called. It wasn't a holiday. The weather was fine. If they were at a construction site, why hadn't she heard anything?

"Okay, Jake is calling her now." Chris inhaled sharply. "I want you to stay with Travis. As soon as I find Maddie, I'll call. Everything is going to be all right. Understand?"

All right? Her stepfather had hurt her little sister. Nothing would ever be right. But her head bobbed up and down, and her hand dropped to her lap.

Travis took his phone back. He spoke quietly to Chris before hanging up. "I'll take you back to Chris's house. We'll wait for news there."

"No." She clenched and unclenched her hands. She needed to keep her head. For Maddie, she needed to think this through. "Please, can we drive around? We might see something. We might..." She blinked, tears burning the backs of her eyes. "Oh, my God. What has Frank done?"

Travis took her hand, and she held onto him tightly. Her mind was starting to catch up to the evidence, and she almost wished it wasn't. She almost wished she could still live in that blissful confusion of just minutes ago, a place where her little sister hadn't been... hadn't...

She broke. Tears streamed down her cheeks and ugly sobs were torn from her lungs.

Travis pressed her face into his shoulder. "It will be okay," he repeated over and over.

But he didn't know that. He couldn't. When her tears slowed, he pulled back. "We should go back to Chris's."

She wiped her hand under her nose. "I can't just sit and wait."

Travis gave her a measured look then nodded. "Okay. We'll drive around."

They drove in what felt like a random pattern around Jacksonville. Sam didn't complain. She didn't have any better ideas.

Her phone rang. Helen. She pressed ignore.

It rang again. Again, she dismissed the call.

It rang a third time. She cursed and answered it. "I can't talk now. I—"

"I saw Maddie when I was on my walk. She was crying in the car as it drove past. She was with your stepdad, so I didn't call at first, but it's been gnawing on me."

"Where? Where did you see her?"

"Heading east on Court Street, next to Riverwalk Park," Helen said. "She looked so upset. What's going on, Sam?"

"I've got to go." She hung up without waiting for a response. Riverwalk Park. A construction site that was quiet.

Sam pointed. "Turn right here."

"Where?" Travis made a call.

"There's an abandoned construction site on Lincoln." Sam leaned forward, her body urging the car to go faster even though her mind knew it didn't work that way. "They were building a multi-use complex but the excavators found an Indian arrowhead. It halted construction until the city is sure it wasn't a burial site or something." And Frank had known about it. He'd laughed and said he was lucky nothing like that had ever shut him down.

"You get that?" Travis asked into the phone. "We're five minutes out." He nodded. "Got it. See you soon."

"Okay, here's what's going to happen," Travis said after he'd disconnected. "When we get there, you'll stay in the car and I'll make a sweep to locate your sister. We'll wait for the rest of the squad before taking action. Got it?"

She nodded, her gaze focused ahead.

Travis pulled into a spot on the street one block down.

Sam threw open the door, ignored Travis's yell, and took off like the hounds of hell were after her.

Her sister needed her. She wasn't waiting a minute longer to find her.

Chapter Twenty-Three

"YOU HAVE EYES ON them?" Chris asked in a low voice.

"Yep." Travis was on the roof of a neighboring building. "I just wish I had my rifle."

Him and Chris both. He could use the talents of One-Shot right about now. But there were a lot of things he was wishing for. That he'd been on base when the call came in so he could have brought more than just his sidepiece. Their comms units would have helped. A mic and micro camera to know what the fuck was happening on the top floor of the half-built structure would have topped the list.

His stomach churned. No, if he had a magic genie, having Sam and Maddie safe right now would have been at the top of his wish list. Travis had seen Frank Saunders on the third floor. Unfortunately, so had Sam, who had raced up the stairs to join the party.

Chris, Jake, Ryan, and Tony were on the ground floor, waiting to move. The building had been framed in with a mix of steel and wood support beams, but construction had halted before the walls had gone up. Which meant Travis could see everything that happened on the third floor.

It also meant Saunders would be able to see them coming.

A raised voice drifted down from above. Saunders was agitated, which could be a plus or a negative. Agitated people weren't thinking clearly; they made mistakes. A good thing when trying to rescue hostages.

Agitated people weren't rational and were hard to predict. Not a good thing.

"He pulled a sidearm," Travis murmured. "Not pointed at anyone yet. Waving it around like an idiot."

Chris inhaled sharply and relayed the information to the other men. "Give the sit reps to Psych from now on," he told Travis. "I'm going in." He disconnected.

Jake stepped between him and the stairs. "Callum and Jakov are on their way with toys. We wait until we're fully loaded before going in."

Chris felt his body temperature spike. He was grateful the men from Delta squad were coming, but he wasn't willing to wait. Calling in the police had been quickly discussed and dismissed. Local PD didn't have the training the Raiders did. Besides, if anything happened to Sam or Maddie, Chris didn't want the police interfering with what he needed to do.

He locked gazes with his team leader. "If it was Caroline in there with a weapon on her, where would you be?"

Jake's jaw clenched. He stared at Chris a moment. Two. Then stepped aside. "If you get a shot, take it." And he'd help Chris deal with the consequences. That part didn't need to be said.

Chris nodded, rechecked his weapon, and moved it to the small of his back. He climbed the stairs two at a time, forcing back the panic. This was his job. He trained for similar situations all the time. If he let his emotions gain the upper hand, he'd be no use to Sam and Maddie.

Still, his heart pounded when he poked his head above the third floor.

Maddie sat in a huddled ball at the edge of the west end. Her knuckles were white as she gripped a metal bar of the scaffolding that had been abandoned next to the building, the raised platform loosely bolted to the third floor of the building. Sauders stood over her, his face red as he ranted. Sam had her back to Chris, her hands up in a placating gesture. She took a small step toward Maddie. Desperation was clear in every line in her body.

Chris's muscles tensed. He took one breath then climbed the rest of the stairs, stepping out onto the floor.

Sauders saw him immediately. "Get out! You can't take her. I have the gun."

He waved the small revolver as though that should solve all his problems. And for his sick, crazed mind, it probably did.

"You do." Chris walked slowly forward. "You have control here. I just want to talk."

Saunders narrowed his eyes. He wiped sweat off his brow with the back of his sleeve. "You're damned right I'm in control." He scanned Chris. "Put your gun down."

Chris halted. "What gun?" Twitching muscles, rapidly blinking eyes. Sam's mother wasn't the only one who was using. Frank was high on something, and that something was probably what had given him the deranged idea he could take Maddie without consequence.

"A big military hero like you? Don't tell me you don't have a gun," he screamed.

Chris analyzed the distance between them. He could make the shot, but was he fast enough to draw and take the man down before Frank got a shot off? The barrel of the revolver wavered between him and Sam. Chris would risk it if it was just him on the roof. He wouldn't risk Sam.

"Okay, you win." He turned to the side so Saunders could watch him lift his shirt and take out the weapon with two fingers. Jake would kick his ass when he heard Chris had surrendered his weapon, but there was nothing else for it. He placed his pistol on the dusty floor.

"Kick it to the side," Saunders demanded.

Chris did.

Sam inched closer to her sister. "Give it up, Frank. Can't you see it's over? There are multiple witnesses. The police are on their way. Your only way out is for you to put your gun down, too."

Saunders leveled the sidearm at Sam's chest, and Chris's throat closed. "This is your fault." Frank reached into his pocket and pulled out a pack of cigarettes. He scowled when he saw it was empty and tossed the wrapper down. "Maddie and I were happy until you interfered."

"Happy?" Sam pressed a hand to her abdomen. "You sick fuck. You'll never touch her again. You'll never even lay eyes on her again." She looked ready to claw his eyeballs out herself.

Chris loved her fire. Her protectiveness. But right now it was making her the prime target. He strode forward, his hands up, and like he wanted, the weapon swung back his way. "We all need to calm down," he said in his best soothing tone. It was hard gentling his voice when all he wanted was to rip the man limb from limb. "Why don't you tell me how you think this is going to go, Frank."

The revolver shook. "You and the bitch are going to leave, and I'll explain everything to Maddie." He lowered his free hand and pet Maddie's head like she was a dog. "It will be good again, like it was before. You'll see. We belong together."

The girl hugged the railing of the scaffolding, her body shaking. The metal bar clanked against its bolts.

Chris's ears pounded. His pulse raced. How had he missed it? The man wasn't only a sick perv, he was obsessed as well. Maddie had been acting out, basically screaming for help, and he hadn't seen a damn thing.

"Take your hands off of her." Sam hurried forward, only coming up short when the weapon turned on her again.

Chris side-stepped until he was between Sam and her step-father.

Of course, Sam took that as an opportunity to sidle closer to Maddie, putting her out in the open again.

Chris gritted his teeth. They were going to have a serious talk about her incessant need to put herself in danger when this was all over.

"Chris." Sam's voice wavered. "Please."

He wanted to tell her it would be all right. That he wouldn't let anything happen to her and Maddie. He couldn't let anything happen to them. Because if anything did, it was game over for Chris. All the walls he'd thrown up, all the distance he'd kept in his past relationships, and the Winters sisters had blown his barricades straight to hell.

He needed Sam. Even needed Maddie, too, and the family they could all become, like he needed his next breath. And, it turned out, his need was greater than his fear. He'd risk everything for them. He'd even risk losing them, if it meant he got to hold Sam each night. Got to torture Maddie on the beach. Make them laugh. Hold them when they cried. They were his family. He'd been a fool to deny it for so long.

And he wasn't going to let this asshole hurt his family anymore.

He analyzed his target. Chris had at least thirty pounds on him. Saunders was shifting his weight back and forth. If Chris could hit him when—

Something clattered on the other side of the floor. Saunders swung his weapon. "What...?"

Chris dropped his center of gravity. He launched himself forward. His foot skidded on a two by four. He lurched but kept going. His shoulder hit the man's thighs, and they both went down.

Saunders's back rattled the scaffolding. He pushed away from the edge of the building and swung the revolver around, but Chris was there. He gripped the man's wrist and twisted. Saunders screamed as the weapon fell from his hand. Chris slammed his fist into the man's face. Once. Twice. Only Maddie's whimper stopped him from turning the asshole's face into a meat pie.

Jake, Tony, and Ryan stole toward them, pistols raised and leveled on Saunders. Jake pulled his phone from his pocket. "Target secure. Time to call 9-1-1."

Saunders moaned, making feeble movements. His fight was gone, but Chris searched him for additional weapons anyway. "Clear."

Tony used his foot to slide the revolver away. "Everyone okay?"

Sam practically leapt on Maddie, wrapping her up tight. The scaffolding shivered as Sam rocked the girl back and forth. "Fine. Right, Mad? You're okay? He can't hurt you anymore."

Maddie dug the heels of her palms into her eyes. Her chin quivered, but she nodded. She drew her shoulders back, glared at her stepfather, and slammed the bottom of her boot into his ribs.

Chris pursed his lips. Even from her seated position, Maddie's kick had power. He didn't know all that Saunders had done to Maddie, dreaded finding out, but Chris knew the man hadn't defeated her spirit.

Sam barked out a laugh that held more tears than humor. "Come on, sweetie." She grabbed the railing and pulled her and Maddie to their feet.

Chris jumped forward and pulled them away from the groaning scaffolding. "The guys will take you two out of here. I'll find you after the police get here."

Sam looked like she wanted to argue. She looked between her stepfather and Maddie, her emotions clear on her face.

She wanted to do more than just kick her stepfather, that was clear, but she also wanted to take care of her sister.

Chris leaned down and pressed a soft kiss to her lips. "Go with Maddie. I'll take care of everything here."

Her gaze darted between his eyes. She bit her lower lip then nodded.

Chris brushed his mouth over hers again, needing the connection. So much could have gone wrong.

Fuck it. He hauled Sam and Maddie into his arms and squeezed tight. The backs of his eyes burned. They were safe. And they were his.

He tugged Sam's head back so they were face to face. "I love you. Fuck, I love you so much."

Her face lit up a moment before she scowled. "You're telling me this now? All the time you had available to you at romantic dinners, on the beach, and this is when you decide to admit it? Unbelievable," she muttered.

He pressed their foreheads together, his lips twitching. Nothing would ever be easy with this woman. Everything would be a battle.

He couldn't wait.

One of the guys cleared his throat.

Chris ignored it. He just needed to hold Sam and Maddie a moment longer.

"I can't breathe." Maddie's words were muffled against his shirt, and finally, he pulled back. He tugged on her ponytail as he gave Sam one last squeeze.

"Go," Chris told Sam. "We'll talk later."

Her smile lightened his soul. It was enough to purify even this dirty situation.

Tony followed them down the stairs, but Jake and Ryan remained. Jake's phone squawked, and he put it on speaker. "That was some rescue," Travis drawled. "All the take-down maneuvers we know, and you went with tripping over your own feet. You were lucky you happened to take the bastard down with you."

"Fuck off. I didn't trip." Chris cocked his head and stared at the man mewling on the floor. Prison was too good for him. "Travis, get off the roof. You two go on down and wait for me."

Jake crossed his arms over his chest. "Prison will keep you and Sam apart."

It might be worth it. Saunders had hurt his girls. But perhaps he should be strategic about it.

Saunders's chin trembled. He reached behind him for the scaffolding's railing and hauled himself to sitting. "You can't hurt me," he said over the groan of metal on metal. "Listen to that one." He jerked his head at Jake. "You don't want to go to prison."

Now the asshole had a sense of consequences?

Chris cracked his neck. The urge to do violence was nearly overwhelming. Men like Saunders didn't deserve to exist. Maddie shouldn't have to face being a witness for a trial. He'd almost killed Sam. The reasons to eliminate him were persuasive.

But he didn't want to be separated from Sam. He needed to keep his head. For now.

Saunders pulled himself up. He sagged against the scaffolding, wiping blood from his face.

A high-pitched whine cut through the air. The railing quivered. Metal peeled away from metal.

And Chris didn't say a word. He watched as Saunders staggered, the weight of one foot resting on the raised platform. Watched as the metal bars tore from their bolts. As a flash of panic raced over the man's face.

Chris's foot didn't even twitch to make a move to help.

Saunders's arms windmilled. He reached back for even ground, but it was too late. His momentum carried him off the third floor and onto the platform. The shriek of the scaffolding collapsing drowned out Saunders's scream.

One moment he was there, the next he was gone. A plume of dirt and dust billowed up from the ground.

Chris felt no satisfaction. No joy. Something that needed to happen had happened. He strode to the edge of the building and stared down at the twisted metal impassively. At least he didn't have to risk prison now.

He turned back to his friends. "Well," he said, placing his hands on his hips, "that was the best of both worlds."

Chapter
Twenty-Four

"SAY IT AGAIN." SAM leaned back against Chris's chest. The sand beneath her was cooling as the sun sank low in the sky, but with Chris's arms and legs around her, she stayed toasty warm.

He heaved a long-suffering sigh. "This is getting ridiculous. If I'd known Sam Winters would be so needy, I would—"

"You would have what?" She craned her head around to look at him, arching an eyebrow.

He bent forward and nibbled her lips. "I would have fallen in love with her just the same."

"Damn straight." She sighed happily and snuggled back against him. The beach was getting empty, except for her and Chris's friends. Everyone was safe, there were no immediate crises, so they'd decided to have a beach barbecue. The guys were around the firepit, Jake and Caroline were strolling along the surf, and Maddie and her friends, Bailey and Jayden were playing a cutthroat game of frisbee. Even Helen, Sam's new, personal hero, had joined them, handing out bags to everyone to collect any garbage they saw.

Sam and Chris had found a nearby dune, and Sam was content to sit in Chris's arms and watch the ocean darken.

"How'd Maddie's first session with the counselor go?" Chris brushed a wind-blown strand of hair off her cheek.

"Good, I think." Sam blew out a breath. "She doesn't want to talk to me about it, of course, but she just looks lighter. Happier, like she was before." Her sister would never be the same girl. She'd had to grow up in a way no kid ever should. But she was strong. And determined, Sam thought, to not let their stepfather ruin another moment of her life.

Maddie shrieked, leaping for the frisbee, and faceplanted in the sand.

One side of Sam's mouth edged up. And she was a bit of a klutz. But she'd be all right. Sam would make sure of it.

Their mother was a different story. After learning of her husband's death, and what he'd done to her daughter, she'd spiraled. Sam could only hope this was her mom's rock bottom, that this would be the point where she decided to turn it around. If she asked Sam for help, maybe she'd give it. But she was still angry and hurt and needed to put all her focus into Maddie.

Pretty soon she'd be her sister's temporary legal guardian. At least their mom wasn't fighting that.

A whistle pierced the air. "Yo." Ryan waved. "Helen's bringing out some cookies she made and we have smore's. Get 'em while they're still here."

Maddie and her friends raced to the firepit. The girl knew how fast Chris's friends could smash through food and wasn't going to be left out.

Ryan frowned in their direction. "Trip, you and your girl coming for dessert?"

"Son of a...." Chris tensed behind her. "I didn't trip," he yelled. "Stop calling me that."

She rubbed his leg soothingly, though her hand couldn't feel half as good as his hard muscles did. "It kinda looked like you did." Though what she remembered most about that day was Chris saving them. One of his squad mates had thrown a hammer across the room to distract Frank, and Chris had taken out the threat. That was all that mattered.

"I went low intentionally," he said hotly. His breath gusted against her neck. "That is not going to be my call sign."

Sam decided to keep quiet. Chris had needed to accept a lot of changes lately. From the gleam in his squad's eyes, she knew the nickname was going to be around for a long time. If Chris didn't want to accept that yet, that was okay.

He'd accepted more than enough when he'd finally figured out that life usually didn't go as planned. Case in point, the two of them. Chris not only recognized the depth of what they had, he'd even tried to out-serious her in the relationship department. He'd grumbled for days when she'd moved back to her apartment, wanting her and Maddie to stay at his house.

It had felt too early, and she'd wanted to ensure the most stable environment possible for Maddie.

But soon. She had no doubt that was where she and Chris were heading.

Ryan waved his hand at them in disgust and turned back to the fire.

"You want to get dessert?" she asked.

Chris nuzzled her ear. "I have all the sweetness I need right here."

He might be content, but Sam wanted more. She turned her body so her legs were over one of his thighs, her shoulder notched against his chest. She cupped his head and brought it down. Their lips butterflied lightly over the others' until Chris deepened the kiss.

Yes, this was a much better position to get some of that sweetness. His kiss spoke volumes. It was passionate and tender. Both greedy and giving. This was how they should always communicate. They didn't have the best history when using their words. Although their fights did usually end in the most delicious ways....

A wolf whistle startled her back to awareness. Heat flushed her cheeks until she realized the sound hadn't been directed at her and Chris.

Jake was at Caroline's feet, the surf swirling at his knee as he asked her a question.

"I'll be damned," Chris murmured.

"Does such an overt sign of commitment scare you?" she teased. She wrapped her arms around his neck, her limbs floating up as though weightless. She was thrilled for her friend. She didn't need to watch to know Caroline would say yes.

His blue eyes darkened when he looked down at her. "Not as much as before." He lowered his head.

They weren't there yet, but Sam could see it. Marriage. Babies, Gray hair and wrinkles. Chris would probably be a silver fox. At least, in her eyes he would.

Because that's what love was. She nibbled on his lower lip, delighting in his groan. Love was heat and comfort. Exasperation and protection. It smoothed the edges of someone you thought you detested and made them beautiful in your eyes.

She shifted until she faced Chris and wrapped her arms around his back, holding him as tight as a vine.

And she was never letting go.

<<<<>>>>

Thanks for reading STALKED! I love bringing these sexy, military men to life and can't wait to bring you more hot Raiders. Get BURNT now!

If you can't stand the heat...
When a bullet takes Marine Raider Travis Kowalski temporarily off active duty, he thinks a little R&R with a sexy jam maker is just what the doctor ordered. But he's about to learn that this woman might just be too hot to handle.

Willow Janna has her daughter, her jam and jelly store, and a schedule she won't let anyone mess with. Who has time for dating when she has payroll to file and PTA meetings to attend? But she's never met anyone like this Raider before. He's tenacious, single-minded and is living proof that chemistry is more than just a reaction on her stovetop.

But more than just her heart is in danger of going up in flames. Someone has decided to put her out of business, by any means necessary. Unless she and Travis can discover who's put a bullseye on her back, her life just might go up in smoke.

Meet the men of Alpha Squad. Protective, strong-willed, and tough, they go hard after what they want. And when they set their sights on a woman, they'll use every weapon in their arsenal to make her theirs. Each book in this series is a fast, steamy read, full of pulse-pounding action and sexy times.

Also By This Author

Hunted

Putting Out Old Flames

Under the Christmas Tree

Courting Disaster

All Wrapped Up

Shelter Me

Forever Home

Forever Found

Forever Wild

The Bakeshop at Pumpkin and Spice (with Donna Kauffman and Kate Angell)

A Wedding On Bluebird Way (with Lori Wilde, Janet Dailey, and Stacey Keith)

That Mistletoe Moment (with Cat Johnson and Kate Angell)

About Allyson Charles

Allyson Charles lives in Colorado. She's the author of sexy and funny small-town romances, and steamy and fast-paced military romances. A former attorney, she happily ditched those suits and now works in her pajamas writing about men's briefs instead of legal briefs. When she's not writing, she's probably engaged in one of her favorite hobbies: napping, eating, or martial arts (That last one almost makes up for the first two, right?). One of Allyson's greatest sources of happiness is that she now lives in a city that has a Cracker Barrel.

Allyson Charles also writes steamy historical romances under the name Alyson Chase, and paranormal romances under the name A. Caprice. You can find her at www.allysoncharles.com.

Printed in Great Britain
by Amazon